THE TIME DECEIVER

An Edward Mendez, P.I. Thriller

BOOK 1

Gerard Denza

The Time Deceiver:
An Edward Mendez, P.I. Thriller
Book I

This novel is entirely a work of fiction. The names, characters, and incidents portrayed in it are the work of the author's imagination. Any resemblance to actual persons, living or dead, events or localities, is entirely coincidental.

Cover Art: Book Covers Art.

Also available digitally.

By the same author:

ICARUS: THE COLLECTED PLAYS

RAMSAY

THE TIME DECEIVER

To Cinnamon,
the bravest little cat in the world.

TABLE OF CONTENTS

PROLOGUE

...and when it was morning, the east wind brought the locusts...they covered the face of the whole earth so that the land was darkened...

-Exodus 10: 13, 15

PART ONE: HOWARD'S BAR

CHAPTER ONE
THE IRISHMAN

I WAS sitting in my father's bar downing my third shot of whiskey. It was one of the few pleasures I had in life. Come to think of it, it was the only pleasure I had in life. I enjoyed staring into the shot glass and trying to make sense of the intoxicating liquor. I would place the shot glass at eye level and swirl the liquid around to form an alcoholic whirlpool. Just one more shot. It was a lie that I told myself often just for the sake of telling a lie. Why should I stop drinking when the liquor was free? Now, why the fuck would I do that?

My name is Howard Winter and has been for all of my life. I am German by birth, but was removed from the Fatherland shortly after I was born and placed in this country. My parents are dead. They were the only friends I ever knew. They told me that I should never trust anyone and that the world was a dangerous place.

My mother and father were all too correct. Cynicism, I was also told, was a good mask for fear. I was taught to perfect this art.

Hmm…maybe, I should have called the bar "Howard's Bar?" A place needs a name to have an existence and be noticed just like a man. For now, I call it "The Bar." Not too imaginative, huh? My father would have thought of a better name, for sure.

What I tell you now must be told because it has affected you. I use the past tense because the event has already taken place. It has altered the scheme of things that is referred to as human history. We must move on from this event, if one is able to…to what? Survive? Maybe.

Stories have beginnings and endings. What occurs in the middle is the fabric that is woven to give the garment its shape and distinction. This is not a story that a man conjures up from his imagination. It is the relating of an historical event that has been hidden. It is an event that marked the end of humanity and then the beginning of something evil. I will do my best to tell it.

It took place in New York City. It began with a man, an Irishman. He was a young man whom I came to love and betray. Betray? How in God's name could I do otherwise?

It was past midnight. It was the middle of September and still warm. It was raining. I had locked the front and the back doors. The windows had been shut with only one window remaining opened in the men's toilet. I sat on the edge of the bowl and laughed. I stopped my laughing when I heard a knock on the door. Now, who could that be at this late hour? He was mad, whoever it was. No matter, I had to answer the door for it was not in my nature to leave things unattended.

I pulled up my pants and took a look in the mirror. The sight was not displeasing: blonde hair, blue-eyed, and hard looking. I combed my hair back. Good. I turned away from the mirror and realized that I had left the bathroom door open. I could have been seen from a number of vantage points. What of it? Perhaps, a passerby had seen me relieving myself?

I walked over to the door and flicked open the outside light. My late night visitor was drenched from the rain. It was Sean. I recognized him at once as the tall and strapping, young Irishman. I liked his look: tall, red-haired and lean. I decided to take a chance and let him in.

-Yes? And, what may I do for you at this hour? We are closed for the night. Can't you see that?

Sean smiled, but it was not a nice smile. No. He didn't like my question or tone of voice.

-Your bar was closed, but the bathroom light caught my eye. I saw you taking a leak in the john over there. You oughta' keep the shades down, man.

-Are you a peeping-Tom? You saw me with my pants down? You make me laugh. Now, I think you should leave.

-I'm not even in, man. Let me in for a few minutes, then you can toss me out into the pouring rain.

-Why should I, Irishman?

-You letting me in or what, pal? I'm thirsty. I need a drink to warm me up. I'll even pay for it.

Perhaps, I should have never opened the door that night to let him in. One must make his choices and not look back to brood. What good does it do?

-Come in and sit down. I'll offer you a drink. I like drinking alone, and I confess that I have already had a few. Straight whiskey?

-Thanks. Make it your best.

Sean walked over to one of the tables and sat down. I ducked behind the bar and took out the bottle of whiskey that I had been indulging in. I held it up for Sean.

-You see, Sean, I have been indulging.

-How do you know my name?

Sean was bending over and taking off his wet shoes and socks.

-Making yourself comfortable? Not too comfortable, I hope. You won't be staying long.

-No. Not too comfortable, man, so get off my back. How do you know my name?

-I have seen you in here a few times. I ask questions. I like to know who comes in. You don't come in often. Why not?

I brought the bottle over to the table along with two shot glasses. I handed Sean his glass and poured the whiskey to the brim.

-Good man. And, I don't like crowds.

Sean downed his whiskey in one gulp.

-I will introduce myself. My name is Howard-

-Good. I don't give a damn what your last name is. I'm starting a job tomorrow, Howard, and I need a few drinks to get me through this miserable night. You dig?

-Of course. But, shouldn't you be home resting and preparing for your first day of work? Surely, there are things to be done?

-There are things to be done, but they're being done for me.

-I don't understand you. What is being done for you and by whom?

-None of your damned business. My fault for bringing it up.

I noticed that Sean had a leather briefcase placed between his legs: an executive's briefcase.

-So, you despair about your new job, eh? Is it the lack of freedom that distresses you or, perhaps, it is something else that you don't want to tell me? You can tell me anything.

I poured myself some more whiskey.

-You're cool, Howard. I don't want this job because I don't like mixing with people. I hate people and it's kind of a real effort for me to get along with them. So, I don't even try.

-Will you begin this job with other people? Yes?
-Yes.

-That is good. You will not be alone in your agony.
-In my kind of agony, I'm always alone, man.

The rain came down in torrents outside. I heard thunder. But, it wasn't thunder that I could hear: it was something else…a low vibration which from that night on never quite left my ears.

-Irishman, show me what is in that leather brief-case. Are you taking it to work with you tomorrow? But, that cannot be for it is obviously stuffed with papers and clearly it is the briefcase of an executive.

I leaned forward and placed my drink to my lips. The liquor smelled good.

-It is not yours. You stole it. Now, tell me why.

-Fuck you. You make an awful lot of assumptions, pal Give me another drink. I've still got this chill in me.

-The briefcase, if you please. And, then, you get another drink.

Sean picked up the leather briefcase and flung it on to the table.

-Here. Look at it. Piss in it. I'm thirsty. Start pouring.

-Take off your wet shirt and help yourself.

Sean helped himself to another drink, but he kept his eye on me. I opened the briefcase and reached inside for the contents. It was an old-fashioned type of brief-case with a flip-over latch that could be adjusted to the thickness of its contents. Contained within this case were manilla folders which I took out and placed on to the table in a neat pile.

-Read 'em, Howard.

-These are files on the people whom you will be working with?

-You're sharp, man. Can't put one over on you.

-Sean, tell me why you go to so much trouble to find out about strangers? And, how did you get a hold of it?

-A friend of mine stole it for me: a chick named Melody.

-You mean that you know someone who is already working within the company? How convenient for you to have a friend who will steal documents. These will be missed.

-Yep. But, I don't think Melody is too worried about that because that chick can take care of herself.

-Your girlfriend, no doubt.

-No. And, too bad, I'd like to have her.

-So, she went into an office and helped herself to some documents?

-Something like that. Ah! To what end? Isn't that the next question...Howard?

-But, that is so obvious: to acquaint yourself with some of the intimate details of your co-workers' lives and to have this advantage over them.

-Good! You're not stupid.

-Tell me about Melody. Perhaps, she is the girl for my affections.

-Maybe. Just maybe, she is.

-I tell you what, Sean, tomorrow, which is actually today, I will go with you to your job and meet Melody.

-Open the damn folders and read...Howard. That's what you wanted, isn't it? They're no ordinary folders.

-Look at the time, Irishman. It is already three o'clock. How is it possible that time has slipped by us so quickly? I find that strange.

-Hmm. That is strange...and it's still raining.

-It's as if we have slept for a while and had forgotten that we had slept.

-Oh, man!

-What is it?

-Skip it. You wouldn't get the joke.

-Ah, secrets. Very well, I have my own. What time must you be at work?

-About eight-thirty.

-That doesn't leave much time for sleep. But, I can see that you have no intention of sleeping. You must go home to at least shower, Irishman.

-Yeah, I gotta'. Don't want to stink up the place.

Sean got up and downed the last shot of whiskey. He shoved his wet socks into the back pocket of his pants and slipped on his damp shoes.

-Howard, keep the folders and the case. If you're smart, you'll read 'em and toss 'em. Gotta' go.

-Tell me where your place of employment is.

-Address is in the briefcase, man. And, if you're not there when I arrive, I'm not waiting for you.

-Fair enough. And, now, you had better go home, Irishman.

I closed the door and stood there for a moment to watch Sean walk down the street: a fine figure of a man. The rain outside was now a light drizzle.

I went back to the bar and opened the first of the ten manilla folders and glanced at a few of the names and addresses inside. I drank my whiskey and threw the files into the trash.

CHAPTER TWO
PHANTOM MOON

I LOCKED the door, gave it a tug, and went on my way. I didn't look back. Never look back. Bad habit. Can't relive a past moment…or can you?

The morning air was chilly but bracing. There was no sun and no rays of light to be seen in the sky. I felt beads of sweat on my brow despite the chill. It was a good thing that I had remembered to bring a handkerchief with me. I reached into my jacket pocket to get it. Why was I sweating? What the hell was I nervous about? Was it nerves or fear?

It was then that I saw Sean who was waving to me from across the empty street. I dabbed at my forehead with the handkerchief and was about to shove it back into my pocket when I noticed tiny spots of blood on it. The morning was turning into a damned nightmare.

-Hey, Howard? Come on, man. I've got no time to waste. Let's move!

-Is there blood on my forehead?

-How did you manage that? Did you wear a crown of thorns or something? Is that handkerchief you're using clean?

-I would not carry a filthy handkerchief on me.

-That's cool, so wipe the blood off your face, man, and let's hurry. I don't want to be late. Well...not too late.

-Lead the way, please. I don't know this area of town so well.

-It's just up the block.

Sean and I walked in silence down lower Broadway until we came to John St. It was here that we made a right hand turn down the narrow street. It didn't take us long to reach the office building where Sean would be working. It was a skyscraper that had been built back in the 1920's. How many people had worked there? How many of them were now dead?

-We part company here, pal. Seems like kind of a waste of a trip for you...Howard.

-You are wrong, Sean. I now know why I had to come.

Again, I took out my handkerchief and dabbed at my forehead. Why would the bleeding not stop?

-Okay, quit with the suspense and tell me why you had to come.

-I came here to wait for you and to meet a few of your co-workers. I feel that something significant is going to happen today. No. I lie. What is going to happen is dreadful.

-Are you psychic or something…Howard? You don't look it.

-No. Why do you ask?

-No reason. I'm going. Take good care of yourself. Your forehead is still bleeding, man; but I don't see any cut marks. Maybe you're just one of those lucky people who ooze stigmata. Huh?

-We will see each other tonight at my bar. We will celebrate your first day of work. Okay?

-See ya' later, man. Try putting a bandage on your forehead. Don't want people mistaking you for you-know-who.

I leaned against the brick wall and closed my eyes. I touched my chest just to see if I had remembered to put on my father's silver crucifix that he'd given me for my birthday such a long time ago. The chain was not around my neck. I tried to think of where I had left it. In my back pocket, I felt the crucifix caressing my hard butt. My hand reached for it, but as I was about to take it out, two people approached me. I let the crucifix dangle in my right hand. I wanted these two people to see it and to know that I believed in Him. I placed my hand to my forehead. The bleeding had stopped.

I opened my eyes and what I saw before me was a mother and daughter. It was inconceivable that it should be otherwise. The younger woman had blonde hair and eyes that were perpetually "startled." The older woman was dark haired and the other side of middle-age.

I smiled at them in greeting. The younger of the two women spoke to me.

-I beg your pardon, is this-

-Yes. I can tell you that it is your place of business. You should go up immediately if you do not want to be late on your first day of work.

-But, how did you know what I was going to ask you? Who are you? Will you be starting work today with my sister? Oh, what a lovely coincidence! Rose, dear, you're already made a new friend.

-You assume far too much.

The older woman spoke to me.

-Get a load of him! Well, if you two don't mind, I think I'll be on my way upstairs. So long, sister dear. You coming up, mister?

-No. I do not work here, but my friend, Sean, and his girlfriend, Melody, do.

-Rose MacDonald's the name. And, this here is my kid sister, Irene.

-Howard Winter. I feel as though I know the two of you ladies already. I want you both to come by my bar tonight for a party of sorts. Tell me that you will come.

The younger sister, Irene, clasped her hands in delight.

-Oh, I adore parties! Of course we'll come. Just tell us when to be there and where to go.

-After sunset, Irene. When else would I have a party?

-After sunset, Mister?

Rose looked astonished at what I had just said. She looked up at the sky. Yes. The older and comical sister was perceptive and picked up on what I was hinting at. A sunset was truly a joke for there as yet had been no sunrise. Irene looked up at the sky, as well. She was startled by the utter blackness.

-Rose and I will be there, Howard. I can't quite take my eyes off the sky. I can't see any stars.

Rose tried to laugh.

-I can top that. There's no damned sun in the sky. Howard? Irene? I'm goin' in. At least inside, I can pretend there's a sun shining and that it's daybreak. It looks like it's still midnight. Shit!

Irene and I walked with Rose into the building and down the corridor to the elevator bank. We felt the urge to follow Rose into the car. We said our goodbyes and left the building, instead.

As we stepped out on to the sidewalk, I could see that Irene was becoming frightened. She pulled at her tapestry handbag and tried groping for conversation or the words that would pass themselves off as conversation.

-Allow me to buy you some coffee in the shop across the street. You look as if you could use some, Irene. I think I could use some coffee and something to eat, as well.

I took her by the arm and guided her across the street.

-Irene, can it be that the coffee shop is closed at this hour? Surely, it is their busiest time of day with all the workers coming in. Although, the streets are deserted. We are the only ones here. The city has never been so quiet.

Irene was looking up and down the street. With an effort, she forced herself to look at me. I placed the silver crucifix around my neck. It was the crucifix that I had been holding all this time in my hand.

-Howard, why don't we go back to my place? I'll fix you some breakfast. Would you mind not eating out so much?

-Actually, I would prefer not to eat out. I am sure that you are a good cook, Irene.

-I am. And- and, I want to get off the street! I'm frightened! Where is everyone? And, why is it still so dark?

Irene was the first of us to speak with fear. She gave words and emotion to a formless dread that as yet had no name or origin to which one could take flight from. There was a coldness in our bodies that had taken hold. It was an awful cold that would never leave us.

And, then, in the sky, we saw something. Irene saw it first. It was at that time that I learned of her predilection toward the occult.

The most beautiful moon hovered just above the horizon. It radiated light like a beacon generating its own illumination and not that of the reflected light of the sun. All about this orb was a circle of crystalline light. The sight of this phenomenon did not comfort us.

-It's beautiful, but it's so different. It doesn't look like our moon, but it must be. And, it looks like it's much closer to the earth.

-Yes. I quite agree with you, Irene. It looks as if someone-

-God?

-As if someone had placed a duplicate moon in the sky; but in the process, has attempted to improve upon the original.

-That's it, Howard! There's no man in the moon and there should be one.

-Perhaps, we are now looking at the other side of the moon: the side whose face is turned away from us? Perhaps, that is where the deceit lies?

-Howard, if that's true, that's bad.

-Why? Tell me why that is so bad.

-You're making fun of me; but I'll tell you all the same. It means that the order is wrong with things and that the balance has shifted to the left pillar of Solomon's temple...and that we've somehow been moved with it and that shouldn't have happened. We should be in the center. We *were* in the center!

-What in God's name are you talking about? What has Solomon's temple to do with any of this? Tell me what you are thinking or do you think so little of me?

-I'll just say it, Howard. I'm afraid of them.

-Of whom? Jews? You make me laugh. Why are you afraid of them? And, don't bother to look about for there is no one to overhear us.

-I'll feel better when we get home. And, someone might be listening. You never know. Let's hurry.

-Yes. Let us hurry for I am hungry. And, I want you to explain to me further about Solomon's temple. I am ignorant when it comes to such things.

The two of us walked in silence uptown. There was no activity anywhere. The streets were empty of traffic and the office buildings were dark and deserted. I could feel the strain upon Irene for it was not in her nature to be so silent. My new friend had a need to speak and to have her presence felt by others.

We had turned too many corners to be able to see the moon that had so disturbed us. The tall buildings blocked our view. But, it was rising in the black sky, of this, I was certain. Its movement of relentless silence and the beauty of its pure, white color...and yet a sphere of death or, as we were to learn, far worse.

As we entered Irene's apartment building, she could have sworn that she had "glimpsed" the shadow of a young woman coming down the flight of stairs. I wanted to believe her because I was desperate for the sight of other people. Irene spoke more of this shadow as she prepared breakfast for me.

-I distinctly saw the outline of a woman coming down the front staircase. Her shadow moved across the wall and descended slowly but with a young woman's movements. And, there was something about the outline…it looked old-fashioned, like something out of another era, but not that far back. There was something beautiful and continental about this woman.

-Is breakfast almost ready?

-Yes.

-She was European in appearance, you say? And, from what time period. This may prove important.

-Oh, say 1940 or somewhere around there. It was the hairdo and the cut of the dress: a nice cut, the type that you don't see around too much anymore.

-And, all of this from a shadow? How did you discern so much detail? Are you imagining this or is there something else at work here that you are not sharing with me, Irene?

-I'm intuitive, Howard, and- well, I'll just come out and say it. I do have psychic abilities and they're genuine and intense. That shadow I saw was trying to communicate with us, but for some reason, it couldn't.

-You don't have to defend yourself with me. I was not accusing you of anything. Could I have some coffee, please?

-Oh, sorry. I'll pour you a cup. But, I'll warn you that I make a strong cup of coffee.

-Good. I like things to be strong and definite.

Irene placed a French style cup and saucer before me. We were eating in a small dining area that was just off the kitchen.

-Thank you. Now, you will tell me about your psychic abilities and of what you perceive is going on.

Make a believer out of this simple, Catholic boy. Give me your impressions of our predicament. And, have some of your delicious coffee.

-I'll try.

I leaned forward in my chair to speak.

-Tell me what you need, Irene. Tell me all of your needs and concerns.

-Oh, please eat, Howard. It's your breakfast, really. It's been a long time since I've fed a man.

I thought that Irene was trying to avoid my questions. But, why? They were questions with a purpose to them. Perhaps, she was simply gathering her thoughts.

-I'll need to conduct a seance tonight. I'll need the help of more people, though. Does that surprise you at all?

-Of course not. You and your sister, Rose, will come to my bar tonight. I have also invited my Irishman friend, Sean. He will bring his friend, Melody, who steals documents for him.

-She steals what?

I paused to catch my breath and to avoid Irene's question.

-And, more people will come, I am sure. There will be more than enough people for a seance. Now, tell me: why is there a need for a seance? No! First, tell me of your feelings about today even though so common a word does not fit into our present reality.

-And, neither do you, my handsome friend. You are what's wrong with this day. Oh, this coffee *is* good!

-Oh, and why am I so "wrong?"

-I don't know just yet. I don't understand it, but everything is balanced in the wrong way.

-Now, you've lost me. More coffee, please?

-There's a new, spiritual balance that isn't in harmony with us yet...or just the opposite.

-Is this balance evil?

-It frightens me, but that doesn't mean that it's evil. It just means that I'm-

The piece of toast that Irene held dropped from her hand. She turned from me and stared out the window. The moon was now visible from the living room window. It cast a pale, white light on to a part of the carpeted floor. It was disconcerting, I must admit. The moon's presence had invaded our haven.

-Irene, pick up your toast and finish eating it. You will need your strength for the seance tonight. Assuming, of course, that we are alive by that time.

Irene picked up the toast, spread some butter on it, and nibbled.

-Cheerful thought, Howard. But, why at your bar? I don't think a bar is an appropriate place for a seance. As a matter of fact, there may be a great deal of negativity stored there. Why can't we have it here?

-Not enough space for all the people that will come, and some interesting people.

-So you've said. But, how do you know that they'll show up or even know where to come? Assuming that they'll want to come.

-They will come for they have nothing better to do. Or, should I say that they have nothing left to do? You're leaning forward to ask a question. Ask it.

-Who are you, Howard? And, what exactly do you know?

-I am Howard Winter. I know nothing of this. Look at the time. Look how quickly it goes by. Why is that? I noticed it before at the bar when I was talking with Sean.

-I don't- what was that? I hear someone. They're coming up the stairs. Do you think it's that woman who I saw before?

-I doubt it. It's probably your sister, Rose, coming home. You know, the older sister who you sent out to work. Don't be too upset with her. She had little choice in the matter, I'm sure. Look. I am right. She places her key in the lock.

The door opened and Rose walked in. She looked as if she were ready to collapse, which is what she did. She sat down with a prolonged sigh of relief on to the sofa and threw her pocketbook on the floor.

-Rose, darling, what are you doing home? And, don't tell me that they've given you time off, because I simply won't believe it. And, don't leave your bag on the floor like that.

Rose stared at her sister in childlike defiance.

-Well, dear sister, there was no one there to give anyone any time off. And, if you haven't noticed, the whole damned city is deserted. I tried knocking on some of the apartment doors just now and no one was there.

-Dear Rose, do speak slowly and coherently and try not to breathe so heavily. We do have a guest.

-Well, pardon me for dropping dead! And, no one was in that damned company either except for the nine of us who were starting work today.

-Irene, give your sister some coffee.

Irene poured Rose a cup of coffee and handed it to her.

-Black with no sugar, dear. Just how you like it. Don't slurp.

-Thanks. Well, at first, it didn't seem like anything too bad was going on. When I got upstairs, a few of the others were already there just hanging around the water cooler talking and, then, a couple of other people showed up. And, we waited-

-Yes, dear?

-Good coffee, Irene. And, no one else showed up! It was so quiet. No phones ringing. Nothing going on…just a kind of humming in the air.

-How long-

-Let her continue, Irene.

-We were standing around that damned water cooler and just waiting for no one knew what. Sean tried one of the phones and there wasn't any dial tone. We all tried the phones and couldn't get an outside line. It got kind of eerie, so me and Melody tried another couple of floors and everything was open but there were no people anywhere. We walked around and even went into a few of the offices and no one was there. It was so damned quiet except for that sort of sound that never stopped. It felt like everyone was dead! Me and Melody went back to the others and Sean told us about how weird things were outside: no people and a moon instead of a sun!

-How did Sean know that?

-Go on, Rose, you are doing splendidly.

-Well, handsome, Sean told us about your little party tonight and we all agreed to meet there at your place at around eight o'clock. We couldn't think of anything else to do except to go on home. We couldn't get out of that place fast enough! You should have seen us all run for the elevator.

Irene sat back in her chair and looked out the window. The moon had passed its zenith and was beginning its descent toward the horizon. The three of us looked at the descending orb. The air was still and there were no sounds, except for that almost imperceptible vibration. If I spoke, the sound would be gone. I did not speak.

CHAPTER THREE
THE SURVIVORS

AFTER LEAVING Irene's place, I took a look at the staircase where the "shadow" had appeared. I couldn't see anything, but I had the distinct impression of someone lurking about. This wasn't a "shadow," it was something real but unseen...hidden. I lingered on the steps for a few minutes touching the iron bannister. Nothing. I saw nothing. I moved on.

I had a few calls to make before the party could begin at my bar. My first stop was to a Frenchwoman's place. I had gotten her address from Sean's files. She was one of the people with whom Sean was supposed to have started work with today.

Impatience and fear propelled me forward faster and faster along the deserted sidewalks. I glanced up at the moon that was descending more rapidly than it had risen. Was it getting closer to the earth or was that my imagination playing a not so funny trick on me? Time was growing short as the shadows of buildings lengthened and reached out toward me. Shadows that were devoid of any light. Soon, darkness would close in.

I reached Yvonne's apartment building struggling for breath and, for a moment, stared upward. There were no lights on in any of the windows except for one. I walked into the building, crossed the lobby and hurried up the stairs. My heart was pounding in my chest as I pressed the door's buzzer. I heard footsteps inside. I assumed that it was Yvonne. The thought of human company made her hurry. I was glad of that. A woman in her thirties opened the door. Her light, brown hair was shoulder length which added height to her petite figure.

-Mon Dieu! Come in, please! I don't know who you are and I don't care.

-I am Howard Winter. Perhaps, Sean has mentioned me to you? You started working with him today. You are to come to my bar this evening.

-Howard, of course, I will be there. Sean did mention you. Now, please sit down and let me offer you a drink. I've already had one myself for all the good it did.

-Whiskey, straight. And, then, I must go.

-No! You must take me with you, Howard. I can't bear to be alone! I will go quite insane. I don't care where it is that you go, but rest assured that I will be with you.

It would be amusing to have Yvonne along, but it wouldn't do. I had to see a Mr. Max Dexter next and Yvonne would only slow me down. She handed me the shot glass.

-Yvonne? Good whiskey. I can't have you come with me, I'm afraid; but, I will see you a good deal of the way to my bar. You were the furthest in distance and I thought that I would work my way back toward the bar.

-Give me a few moments and I'll be ready. Don't leave without me, I beg of you.

The frenchwoman hurried back into her bedroom to change. I got up and helped myself to some more whiskey. I decided to drink it straight from the bottle rather than to dilute its flavor. Yvonne kept a nice apartment with all of the appropriate knickknacks and photographs displayed in the right places and at the most flattering angles. I saw that the kitchen was off to my right. I called out to her:

-I think we should pack some food for tonight. Do you have a picnic basket?

-Yes! It's in the cabinet, Howard. Take it and stuff it with food and wine. Take whatever you want.

-I will get the basket; but, you will pack the food. I trust more to your judgment than to mine. Are you almost ready?

-Yes. I am hurrying.

Yvonne walked out of her bedroom tying a black scarf about her neck. Her make-up had been freshly applied and she wore flats with a full cut skirt. She carried her purse in her right hand.

-I will see to the food. My shawl, Howard; I left it on the bed. Would you please get it for me? The heat hasn't come up all morning. Such a ghastly chill in the air!

Carrying the bottle of whiskey, I walked into the bedroom and scooped up the shawl. I laughed. I was getting an erection at the sight of a woman's bed.

-Yvonne, are you ready? It is time for us to go. I will walk with you most of the way and, then, you must continue on to the bar by yourself. Do you think you can manage it alone?

-Yes.

-You don't sound so certain about that. Come on. Let's be on our way.

Yvonne walked in carrying the picnic basket which looked heavy. I took it from her and handed her the woolen shawl. I kept the bottle of whiskey in my other hand. No more words passed between us as we left her apartment. She locked up the place and drew her shawl about her shoulders. She slipped her arm through mine and we walked toward my bar. All the time, she stared up at the moon as though hypnotized by its brilliance. If she stared at it too long, would she be placed in a trance?

-Yvonne? I wouldn't stare at that moon if I were you. It might not be healthy.

-You are right, Howard. Its light is almost blinding. It doesn't even look like our moon.

-Look. I must leave you here, my sweet, to continue on your own. Can you manage the basket by yourself? I'll take it with me if you can't.

-I hadn't thought of that. Is it much further, Howard?

-Five blocks more in a straight direction and one block to your left.

-I don't think that I can manage it. Please, forgive me-

Yvonne stopped speaking in mid-sentence. A movement in the near distance had caught her attention.

-Mon Dieu! Becky is coming, and she will help me. I would have surely died walking by myself. I am not strong, and I admit it.

A young girl ran up to us with her long, dark blue dress billowing about her legs. I was struck with the impression of a fifth grader. She was neither slim nor fat, but her pixie hairdo accentuated her chubby cheeks and even her manner of speaking had a school girl's air to it.

-Oh, Yvonne, I thought I'd just die if I stayed at home by myself. I just had to come out because I knew at least Howard- Oh, hi! I'm Becky. I knew that Howard would be at the bar, and I needed to have at least one drink even though I can't hold my liquor, but at least there would be somebody there to talk to and I'm so glad that I ran into you two guys because I hate walking into a strange place by myself.

I interrupted her.

-Pleased to meet you, Becky. Yvonne, I am glad that you have company. I must proceed in a different direction. Go directly to the bar. I will join you there later. Don't make any side trips.

I took my leave. In a short time, I would learn that Becky was a sensitive and an innocent. I watched the two of them walk down the street with each one grabbing a handle of Yvonne's picnic basket and gaining a certain measure of strength from the other's presence.

I walked to Max's place still holding the half empty bottle of whiskey. It was fortunate for me that I had worn my old, comfortable white sneakers which went well with my dark blazer and slacks. I buttoned up the top button of my white shirt even though I wore no tie.

In a few minutes, I stood in front of Max's building. It was the same as Yvonne's place: deserted. I rang the doorbell and never let it be released until he answered. A man who might be hiding, must be forced out into the open.

-Do you want something or are you selling?

Max was older than I had imagined. He stood well over six feet in height, but erect and with an athletic build. At one time, he must have been an athlete.

-Actually, a little bit of both. Let me in, please. I have a few things to tell you.

-I have noticed the rather unusual moon and there doesn't seem to be any sun in the sky which is a bit unnerving. And, the darkness doesn't seem to be giving way to light. You wouldn't be Howard, by any chance? Sean did mention something about a party and free drinks.

-Invite me upstairs and we can finish off this bottle of whiskey together. Yes. I am Howard Winter.

After a few drinks, Max and I walked in the direction of my my bar. The two of us felt the moon's presence as it ripped a path for itself through the black sky. It was making its maiden voyage, but toward where?

-Do you hear that humming sound, Howard? It never stops and its always on the same frequency. You do hear it? It isn't my imagination, is it?

-No. And, it's annoying. It has been mentioned by others.

-Speaking of others, Howard, look down there. We've got company.

A short distance from us stood two men. I placed my arm on Max's shoulder to stop him. I wanted these two men to approach us. In a moment, they did. A handsome boy of about sixteen came forward. He was not as tall as I, but he carried himself with confidence. His companion was an Hasidic Jew whose appearance baffled me, for I did not understand the reasoning behind it. His long, black great coat and side curls were annoying.

The young boy spoke to us.

-I'm glad we bumped into you guys. It's kind of lonesome out here with nobody out doing anything. I hooked up with Abraham and, man, was I glad for the company. The entire city's like some kind of a ghost town with no traffic and no people. What the hell is going on?

Max started to speak, but I cut him off. My questions had to be asked and answered quickly.

-You know each other, but surely you are not friends?

Michael, that was his name, grew flushed with anger. His voice was harsh, but controlled when he answered.

-Yeah. We're friends, man, and what's it to you? The two of us were starting a work program today, but things got kind of strange, so we decided to hang out-

I interrupted this pathetic speech.

-No more of this small talk. All of us must go to my bar now before that phantom moon sets. God only knows what will happen then.

-Howard, there's someone else in the shadows over there: another member of our little party, no doubt. Shall we greet him?

-Why not, Max? He may know a few things that we do not.

The shadow within the shadow moved. It knew that we had seen it emerge from its black hole. An Asian man walked toward us. He wore a black kimono that reached down to his feet. His hands were folded in

front of him as if in prayer. He could have been any-where between twenty-one and forty.

-My name is Howard Winter. Who are you, please, and how do you come to be here?

-My name is Oshido Tsu. I have heard about your impending ritual for this evening through my co-work-ers. I have no answers to give you regarding our pre-sent situation. However, I do offer myself as a participant even though a seance can be dangerous..

I smiled at him.

-I like you, Oshido. You're intelligent and humble.

-Thank you. We must depart for your bar at once. How kind of you to offer it as a refuge to us, for I fear that the true terror of this endless night has yet to un-fold.

CHAPTER FOUR
OUTCASTS

THE FIVE of us men walked to my bar: the refuge, as Oshido had called it. Why did the use of that term disturb me? I had no real knowledge yet of anything and there were the others to keep me company, but it wasn't enough. We were all so submerged in ignorance that almost any course of action would have been welcome.

As we walked uptown, the only sound in the entire city were our footsteps on the pavement. The street lights were working, but the light that they cast didn't make it to the sidewalk. I could only see a few feet in front of me.

I stole glances at Abraham. His presence had touched a raw nerve; so raw that I had to control a murderous rage.

At last, we arrived at our refuge. Oshido had been correct. His simple phrasing and clearness of vision had much to say for itself. I held the door open and allowed them to pass through.

Sean stood behind the bar and helped himself to the whiskey. He had appointed himself bartender, which was just fine with me. He waved me over and poured a shot for me. I noticed that there was a third glass on the counter filled with nothing but ginger-ale. Sean caught this and cracked a grin across that ruddy, handsome face.

-It's Melody's. The chick doesn't drink, man. She's in the ladies room. Have a drink...Howard. You look like you could use one.

-Cheers, Irishman. And, you are right. I needed this. So, tell me what you've been doing all this time: getting acquainted with the women?

-There's only one woman I want to get to know.

-Melody? Should I even guess?

-You should know, man. She's worth that erection you're playing with now.

-You are truly disgusting, but I appreciate what you say. I am erect.

-You're cool...Howard.

-Another drink, if you please.

-Thinking of beating up the Jew boy? You keep staring at him like you want to. Do it, Howard. Knock his teeth down his throat. What are you waiting for?

-Perhaps.

-Well, look who's coming.

I turned around and stared at the woman who came toward us. I had never seen a woman as beautiful as she. Her eyes were aquamarine. Her hair was strawberry blonde and shoulder length. The figure was sensual, but in no way vulgar.

-You must be Howard. I'm Melody.

Melody extended her hand and I touched it with both of mine. Her scent was deep and crisp and with a hint of the ocean breeze to it. I wanted to bury my mouth in her neck and kiss her roughly, but not too roughly.

-Thank you for this refuge, Howard. I don't know what we would have all done otherwise.

Again, that term "refuge." I glanced toward one of the windows. The moon's light streamed through and "crept" along the floor like a living presence that sought to invade our refuge. Yvonne, who had been watching Melody, followed my glance. She stifled a gasp. She got up and pulled the curtains closed.

-I was only too pleased to be of some aid, Melody. What else could I do under these strange circumstances?

Sean poured me another drink and freshened Melody's. She ignored the Irishman.

-We've a long night ahead of us, Howard. But, the time will pass quickly...too quickly. I shouldn't laugh. Chalk it up to nerves. Sorry.

Melody had a charming laugh and more than one person in the room turned to look. It was the first laughter that we had heard for what seemed like a long time.

-Have you spoken to Irene, yet? She will be conducting the seance. It was her idea, you know. I've never been to one myself.

-Yes. She's lovely. She seems to know a good deal about ritual and the occult. We can trust her, Howard. We have to.

-We have no choice, is what you mean. Anyway, I sense that you also are gifted.

Melody stirred the ice in her drink before responding.

-I am a psychic, but it's a gift that seems to come and go of its own accord. I am sensitive in feeling the needs and moods of people; and this I do control, probably because I want to.

-Good. It's a gift that suits you well.

-I haven't really thought about what's happened today. It's difficult to take it all in. I am starting to think about it now, though.

-So, tell me, Melody, have you drawn any theories or conclusions. What are your feelings on things as they stand? Are we the only survivors left of the human race?

-I don't know. All of us must be responsible for this in some way or else we wouldn't be here...wherever "here" is. Howard, are we still in the same city? Is this New York City? Do you know? Have you guessed or has anyone guessed?

-I doubt it.

-I'm sorry. I'm asking a lot of questions and not giving any answers. I do know that I was awake all of last night if that means anything.

-That's interesting, Melody and, perhaps, it is a beginning. I did not sleep either and neither did my Irishman friend here. And, another interesting point that you raise: the question of responsibility. There is someone responsible for our being here and surrounded by darkness and a phantom moon. I am glad that you raised that point: the question of who is behind it all. And, as to where we are, Irene has already given a clue as to that; although, she didn't realize it at the time.

Irene came over to the bar and stood between Melody and me. She was agitated.

-Did I hear my name mentioned? How flattering.

-Irene, have you not told Melody and the others where we find ourselves trapped?

-I wasn't aware that I knew, Howard.

Irene behaved like a jealous woman. Melody did not anger her, but it was my being so close to Melody that did. It was Melody, however, who soothed Irene's hurt feelings where as I would have done the opposite.

-Please tell us, Irene. If we know where we are, at least that would help the seance tonight. We wouldn't have to grope about so much or at least it would be one less unknown to come to grips with.

-All right, I will tell you, dear. Oh, bartender? A gin and tonic, please, with a slice of lime, of course? Thank you.

Melody still did not acknowledge Sean. I spoke to him. Irene had just spoken to him. But, for Melody, he simply did not exist.

Sean handed Irene her drink. She stirred it with delicate and ladylike gestures, never lifting her eyes from it. At last, she spoke to her captive audience.

-I couldn't help but overhear some of your conversation just now. Of course, I wasn't actually eavesdropping; but, I did manage to catch an occasional stray word. I didn't sleep a wink myself last night, partly out of choice and partly out of- well, we won't get into that just now. It never stopped raining and time was behaving oddly. It seemed to slip out of its linear dimension. It wasn't obeying man's restrictions on it any longer. Our imposed measurements no longer held it captive like some criminal or slave. In short, my sweets, this precious thing which we call time can no longer be measured or even casually referred to. It's no longer the comfort or restraint that it once was.

-That was a good speech. We believe you, Irene. Now, would you please answer yet another question for us? Where the hell are we?

Irene turned to look out the window, but Yvonne had drawn the drapes on all of them and was now talking to Becky and Abraham.

-That's more difficult to answer, Howard. I think that I may have a clue. That middle drape will have to be drawn open later.

-What is this clue that you speak of, Irene? Tell us.

Sean was about to pour more ginger-ale into Melody's glass, but she placed her hand over the top. Yes. Even with that small gesture, she would not acknowledge the Irishman.

-The moon, that horrid piece of rock that's been flaunting itself at us all day long, flaunting its beauty and its prisoners.

-Prisoners, Irene? I don't understand.

-I think you do, Melody. You're afraid, aren't you? I don't blame you. Use your psychic ability, if you dare, and explain a few things to Howard and our bartender, Sean. It's not pretty.

-Irene?

-Yes, Howard, dear? I am answering the questions as best I can. You will allow me to revel just a bit, won't you?

I forced myself to watch Irene sip her gin and tonic or Tom Collins or whatever it was that she had ordered. I wanted to break the glass and kill her.

-I believe that it's the dark side of the moon that's been facing us all day…staring at us and…this is so difficult…something is trying to speak to us. It's that vibration that can't be quite listened to because if you listen to it, *truly* listen to it, you'd be driven insane or worse.

At that moment, we heard that sound which no person can forget once having been exposed to it. It was a cry that came from the outside. It surrounded the building. It sealed us in like nails driven into a coffin. We followed its movement along each of the outer four walls. We listened. No one spoke for any words would have been inconsequential and a useless attempt at courage.

I saw Oshido walk over to the bar. Up until that moment, he hadn't spoken to anyone. He placed several bar stools between himself and us: a physical distance of a few feet which was not intended as a slight. It was a space for himself that he needed and that he took. Oshido did not face the bar, but faced us, instead. Sean walked over to him.

-Can I help you, pal?

-Scotch, please.

-Straight up, man?

-Yes. Thank you.

I raised my drink to Oshido. And, he, being a gentleman, raised his in return. We both drained our glasses.

Michael and Becky walked over and sat down next to Melody. I ordered a beer for Michael and a ginger-ale for Becky. I was running the place and felt that I had to take responsibility for these two young people.

-Thanks for the free beer, man. I sure could use it. That sound outside is getting to me in a real bad way. Any idea what it is?

-You're a young man, Michael, so try not to be too frightened.

-Why shouldn't Michael be scared, Howard? I know I am and I think I know why.

-Tell us, Becky. And, don't be frightened. You're with friends.

-It's not just one sound, Melody. It's so many different voices and they're all so wretched and hating and it makes me afraid to listen because I know that if I really do listen, I'll make out words and people. Oh, God! I'll recognize voices. I just know I will!

Rose ran up to Becky to comfort her. Rose was not the maternal type, but she was a good-spirited person who was fun to be with because she was a self-made clown. On her way to consoling Becky, she had knocked over her beer glass and spilt good liquor on to the floor.

This now left only three of our number not at the bar: Max, Yvonne, and Abraham. As if reading my thought, Max walked over to the bar and stood next to Becky and Rose. He ordered a refill.

Now, only Yvonne and Abraham sat apart from us. Yvonne was self conscious of this, but what was she to do? She couldn't bring herself to leave the Hasid by himself and, yet, she was aching for a drink to satisfy her alcoholic desire.

I decided to start trouble and charge the air with action. It would bring people out of themselves and forge allies and drop veils.

-Yvonne, why don't you quit being an outcast and join the party? Sean, pour Yvonne a double vodka; but, don't bring it to her, let her come and get it…that is, if she can pry herself from her Jew boyfriend.

Becky had recovered sufficiently to throw a retort at me.

-Oh, Howard, that's not nice. Abraham's not doing anything to you so why don't you leave him alone? You're a bully. Don't we have enough to be scared about already? All that sound out there and the dark-ness and haven't you noticed that it's getting darker in here? Why can't you just leave people alone?

-Shut up. What's out there doesn't concern me right now.

-And, leave Yvonne alone, too. Maybe, she just wants to sit there with Abraham? Did you ever think of that? I'll bet that you didn't.

-You have a big mouth, Becky. Shut up.

-Hey, man, don't talk to her like that. You listening to me?

I could have lifted Michael from his stool and beaten him to a pulp. But, for the moment, I would let things stand. Then, I would ignite them into flames…burning and hateful flames. My objective was to get the remaining people to the bar.

-Yvonne, your drink is waiting for you. Perhaps, you will send your boyfriend over for it. If he were a gentleman, he would be on his way here now to fetch it for you. Apparently, he is no gentleman.

The effect that this had on Yvonne was strange. She stood up and placed her shawl about her shoulders de-fiantly and beckoned Abraham to follow her to the bar. I know why she did this. Of course, being a woman she would not thank me for the favor that I had just done her. She was frightened to be by herself, and Abraham's presence frightened her even more because of unsaid things and unguessed at mysticism which she knew he represented. It terrified her being in that part of the bar with such a man.

And, now, we were all at the bar with a drink in front of us or held in a hand ready to be gulped down. Before I started more trouble, I had a few questions to ask and a few statements to make.

-I am curious. Has everyone here not slept the previous night? Do we all share that in common?

To my surprise, it was Abraham who answered.

-I overslept. I am a sound sleeper, but my dreams were disturbing.

-I don't care about your damn dreams.

-Howard?

-Yes, Max?

-I had no trouble sleeping, either. Why do you ask?

-I am looking for a common thread. There has to be a reason why we're here.

Michael spoke. He held his half finished beer in his hand.

-I've always been a loner, but nothing like this. Even my parents-

-Go on, say it! I feel that it is important.

-Don't rush me, Howard. My parents kept away from people and encouraged me to do likewise.

-Strange advice to give to a young man. Why?

-Don't pressure the boy, Howard. Let him talk.

-Very well, Melody.

-My Mom and Dad were kind of afraid of other people. I never really knew why. It was after the war when it started. I heard my parents talking about being trapped in a bomb shelter for a couple of days and that's where they first met. I wish I knew more.

-Howard, my own parents spoke of something quite similar to Michael's parents' experience.

-Tell us about it, Yvonne.

-It was also after the war when things were still unsettled in France. My parents had been trapped in an underground vault. They thought that they were going to die, but they were saved at the last moment just when the air was about to run out. It was strange. I remember my mother saying that the people who rescued them were somehow different...almost menacing, even though they had been her co-workers for many years.

Max downed the rest of his drink and spoke up. His speech was a little slurred, but intelligible enough.

-Howard...everyone...I was a young boy just when the war had ended. I remember how brutal the winter had been. But, the spring was lovely. It was on a spring day when I quite accidentally locked myself in an old bomb shelter just outside of London. It took me the better part of a day to get myself out, but-

-Continue, Max. Your story is sobering you up.

-I heard strange noises...horrible sounds, really. I was almost afraid to come out. Afterwards, things seemed quite odd. It was as if the world had quietened down to a silence that one could almost feel. It was quite ghastly. And, everyone seemed different. I can't really explain how.

Irene spoke. She had downed her gin and tonic and was staring into the empty glass.

-Howard? Everyone? My sister, Rose, and myself have always been, shall we say, set apart from other people? I've always been uneasy around others. I really don't know why. It might explain my being such a bohemian. Rose, dear?

-Irene's right. Our mother and father were almost recluses. They never went out, at least not if they could help it. The blinds were always drawn, the door always locked. We weren't allowed to go to school like the other kids or even play with them. We never had any visitors.

-That would explain your own eccentric behavior, Rose.

-Don't be a smart aleck, Howard.

-But, we are all eccentric, Rose. Becky? Melody? Oshido? Sean? Have you or your own relatives shared similar experiences?

Sean spoke up from behind the bar.

-Leave me out of this, man. I didn't get any sleep last night, remember?

Melody spoke.

-I didn't sleep, either, Howard. But, all my life, I've felt separated from other people. It was as if they felt me watching them.

-Were you?

-Yes, Howard, I was. I don't know why. It just seemed that I was an observer who had been placed in a strange land as an outcast.

Becky blew her nose and spoke.

-Oh, Melody, that's just how I've always felt, except for a feeling of resentment and-

-And, what Becky?

-Hatred. I felt their hatred, Howard. It was a hatred that was brewing just beneath the surface. It makes me scared to even think about it.

Oshido put down his drink and addressed the group.

-Outcasts. That is what we are. All of us have been outcasts all of our lives. Isn't that what you have been getting at, Howard? Either we or our parents experienced something dreadful. I will relate a brief experience of my own. Like Max, I, too, was alive after the war. I was living in SanFrancisco with my family. We were visiting my uncle's antique store. Somehow, I wandered into the back room and found myself going into his storeroom in the basement. An unusual Chinese trunk caught my attention. It had been placed in an upright position. You would call it an armoire. It was opened and I decided to climb in.

Oshido took a deep breath and continued with his story.

-Once inside, the lid slammed shut and I was trapped. My first impulse was to call out for help, but something cut short my breath. I heard terrible noises outside. I could make out people screaming and running in the streets above. I was frozen with horror. Had the city been invaded? Had something descended from the sky to wreak havoc? I put my hand to my mouth to stifle a cry. Was it the end of the world? I dared not move. And, then, I heard something crawling...yes...crawling down the stairs as if it were looking for me. I heard- no- felt this thing crawl along the trunk attempting to open it, but this thing could not release the mechanism. I wanted to cry out in terror, but could not. And, then, a silence descended. It was a silence that was shattering. It was the most dreaded silence in the universe. Life on this planet had been obliterated. I am certain of this. And, then, I could hear movement once again. It was as if life had come back to the wor ld.

-Oshido? Who let you out of the trunk, man?

-I managed to release myself, Sean. I found the hidden mechanism. I went back upstairs and I saw my mother and father and uncle cleaning up debris. I don't know what else to call it. It frightened me. *They* frightened me.

-Had your relatives seemed changed in any way?

-You ask perceptive questions, Sean. Yes. They *were* changed. The images before me were not my parents. I know this. But, I dared not voice my thoughts.

-Well, something happened, that's for sure.

-I agree, Sean. But, what?

Irene, who was rummaging in her "carpet" bag, spoke without looking up.

-An Armageddon so horrific that we can't even imagine what it could have been. I think the year it might have occurred was 1947. Yes. That must be when it happened. I'm sure of that.

-When what happened? Please tell us, Irene.

-I don't know, Yvonne. I don't know. I don't want to know.

Max, who had ordered another drink from Sean, spoke to the group at large.

-Well, luv, we'd better bloody well find out. You're right about the year, Irene. That's just about when my little experience occurred. It gives me the willies just thinking about it.

Oshido looked at each of us in turn as he spoke.

-My first thought when I awaken and my last thought before I sleep is of that horrible day.

The mood was too tense. I decided to cause trouble and awaken the others from their reverie and their fears.

-So, tell me, Michael, do you have a girlfriend? Have you screwed her, yet? Assuming, of course, that you are big enough.

-You bastard!

Michael reached over and tried to grab me. Sean stopped him and pinned his arm to the bar.

-Take a joke, man, and cool off. Howard, here, didn't mean anything by it. Did you...Howard?

-Tell him to lay off me, Sean.

-Just cool it for now.

Yvonne spoke to us in a slow, but angry, voice.

-I grow tired of these games. You bore me, Howard. You are not at all clever because you are so damned obvious. Yes. I see through you. We've more important things to discuss, eh? Why did you change the subject? Mon Dieu! Not even this shawl can keep the chill from seeping through! This cold is quite ghastly. Have any of you noticed?

Yvonne was right. The air was cold and stagnant. It hung about us and penetrated us to the bone.

-Yes.

Abraham had an opinion...interesting.

-I'll say! The lights are on, but its getting darker. Maybe, the electricity's starting to go? That's *all* we need!

-Dear Rose, please don't start a panic. The electricity is not going but, perhaps, candles are what's called for and even a lantern? Sean, be a lamb and look behind the bar for these few articles, would you? And, by the way, does anyone have the time?

Before answering Irene's question, Max gulped down his drink: his third? his fourth? I lost count.

-It's just half past nine, Irene. I think.

Sean looked up from the bar.

-The only thing behind this bar is liquor, Irene. Maybe, my friend can find us some candles? How about it...Howard?

-There are some candles in my room upstairs and an oil lantern. Wait a few moments, and I will get them. I haven't finished here yet.

Rose looked up and strained her neck over the bar to face me. Her face was flushed with defiance. It was the defiance of a simple-minded child who is about to erect a defensive wall about herself that a lighted match would incinerate in a second. She began her tirade which was loud and clear and directed at me.

-Hey, I'm sick of listening to you, Howard. Maybe, you can pick on poor Abraham and get away with it, but you can't get away with that crap with me!

I laughed long and hard.

-But, Rose, I have not chosen to insult you just yet. I thought that I would incite your sister, Irene, to do that for me. I am sure that she could do it far more effectively.

Rose's bloated face grew a shade redder as she turned to her sister.

-What have you been telling him, Irene? Bitch!

-Why nothing at all, dear. And, if you all don't mind, I think I'll remove myself from this little group scene. I've more important things to think about.

-But, I would mind a great deal, Irene. I want you to stay and enjoy the party. No one will leave the bar until I give them permission to do so.

-And, who in hell died and left you boss? Howie-boy's taking over the joint!

-Are you a strong woman, Rose? And, please tell us why you have never married for surely there were offers.

-I am strong. I am strong!

Sean was laughing his damned head off.

-Careful, man, you're gonna' knock over your friend's drink.

Irene tried to intercede.

-Rose dear, please try not to make a spectacle of yourself. We really have much more important things to worry about. And, why do you let Howard goad you on? You are a child.

Oshido spoke from his end of the bar. He was not pleased with our behavior.

-Stop this at once. You are accomplishing nothing by these games. We have much to do before we reach the midnight hour when, in all likelihood, the moon will set. Perhaps, you haven't thought of that occurrence, but I have given it a great deal of thought. What will happen when it occurs? Can anyone answer that? No. I have no answers, either, except that we must begin our seance before midnight. We must also establish questions before we can seek answers.

-What are those questions, Oshido?

-Where are we and what has become of all other living beings, Melody. How did we come to be here and what force or purpose has brought us together? We are all outcasts in some sense of that term. Perhaps, we were brought here to be eliminated? Perhaps, we are a threat to someone? There are more questions to be asked, but those are the ones that we must answer.

-Oshido is right, Howard. We can't begin to do anything unless we have a sense of what's happened to us.

-You are right, Melody. Or should I say that Oshido is right? I have been wasting time. Sorry.

Max, who was still sober, spoke to me.

-You haven't been wasting our time so much as filling it, Howard. We're trapped here now and I don't see any means of escape...escape from what and into what? And, that noise out there is terrifying, rather.

We listened with the darkness creeping in about us and the hell voices outside becoming more distinct.

Abraham spoke, but it was difficult to hear him.

-All this should not be happening to me. This morning, I went to synagogue and said my prayers. I have nothing to atone for, so why is it that I am- I do not know. I was late for temple, but my intent was there.

-Just as I thought, Mr. Abraham places himself above us all. He shouldn't be here? But, you are here, Hasid! You are here with us and so no further pretense is necessary.

-Dear Howard, how you delight in upsetting us all. However, Abraham has just found the common thread that may have acted as a spiritual catalyst in bringing us here.

-Get a load of my crummy sister!

-You've recovered your wits, Rose? How fortunate for us, dear sister. But, as I was just saying, most of us didn't sleep last night and there must be some significance in that.

Yvonne emerged from her half-drunken stupor.

-Hmm...I wonder.

-Yvonne, what is it that you wonder. Perhaps, the alcohol has enlightened your perceptive powers?

-Oh, you're so mean, Howard.

-Don't talk to him, Becky. Don't pay any attention to him.

-Your boyfriend, Michael, orders you about?

-No one orders me about, Howard. Go to hell!

-I wonder…

-Yvonne, spit it out, please. Sean, pour Yvonne another drink. Perhaps, she needs to be drunker, still?

Yvonne spoke up with a look of realization in her eyes.

-I wonder if we're all dead? It is a possibility, no? Perhaps, we are in purgatory.

-I don't think we are. I still have that sense of hope that the answer is so simple, but still so awful.

-Death is simple, Melody. That is why I state it. If we're dead, we're dead and there's nothing more to say. That's it. Where is my drink, bartender? How shabbily you all treat Yvonne. Pity me! I need a drink!

-We may have been cast on the other side of the glyph.

-Eh? What are your saying, Abraham? I have heard of this glyph: this Jewish symbol. Tell Yvonne…

I laughed derisively; but, I didn't care.

-The Jew and the drunk! How amusing. Continue and don't let us interrupt you, Yvonne.

-I can't speak of it for I am ignorant of its many complexities. My Aunt Madeline was versed in the Qaballah, Howard. But, she was a secretive and superstitious woman. She didn't trust anyone.

-Continue, Yvonne. Don't let my laughter distract you.

-Yes! That's it! I remember. The glyph that has taken so many forms throughout history. The Tree of Life in the Garden and there was something else…my aunt spoke of it once, but the memory fades. It took other forms, as well… evil, living forms. What was it? The other side of life: the Qlipthoth! The dark side of the universe.

We were silent for a few moments. Melody broke this silence.

-It's past ten o'clock, Howard. I'll help you find the candles and the lamp. Let's hurry.

Oshido was the first to leave the bar. He sat down in the far corner and assumed an asana position: the lotus position with his right hand placed within his left.

Irene made her way through the darkening room until she found the chair where she had placed a small but comfortable cushion. Gently, she sat on it. I gave out a laugh. Was her backside made of fine crystal? How delicately she placed her rump on to the chair.

Max stayed at the bar. He felt comfortable there and, with Sean behind the bar, he would not be alone. He decided to strike up a conversation.

-Sean?

-What's on your mind, Max?

-If it's none of my business, just tell me.

-Keep talking, man.

-Are you married?

-No.

-Do you live with family.

-No.

-When I met you at work today, you just didn't fit in with the corporate structure. I say that as a compliment because as a bartender, you're quite yourself.

-Meaning?

-Oh, I don't mean anything by it, mind you. I was wondering why you would even think of working-

-Hey, Max?

-Yes?

-Mind your own fucking business.

Yvonne sat down next to Max. She also had no desire to leave the bar. The company of two men was not unpleasant to her.

Becky, Michael, and Abraham were about to leave the bar to find themselves a table to sit down at and, perhaps, chat amongst themselves: young people becoming more intimate. I could not allow this. I lashed out at Abraham.

-So, tell me, does Abraham know that he is with a pretty girl? Or does his manhood not know how to respond and grow hard like a man? Perhaps, Becky does not excite him? Michael, get away from those two. I have my suspicions about Becky.

Abraham cowered in the dark. Becky launched a verbal assault, but I heard not a word of it. Michael came flying at me with his dukes up and ready to box. I put up mine and we fought. I threw the first punch and Michael skillfully ducked. He threw a punch and I deflected it. I threw a left-hook and caught him on the jaw. Michael went crashing into a table. Good! I threw my body on top of his and started pummeling.

Everyone crowded around us. Becky cried. Rose cheered Michael on and looked for an opportunity to trip me up. She found none. I saw to that. Max looked to separate us. Irene paid us no attention. Oshido remained silent in his corner. Yvonne kept out of the way. Melody stood near Sean who laughed at us. I knew that Melody waited for an opportunity to separate us.

I grabbed Michael by the waist and threw him and myself against the wall. He lost his cool and missed all of his punches. I liked this boy in spite of everything.

Michael's foot caught on the velvet curtain and it came down on top of us. We were now covered by the soft fabric and this inhibited our fight. We could not see the spectacle that we had just uncovered. The screams stopped our fist fighting.

-That's Becky screaming. Let me up, Howard.

-Wait a moment until the shock at what they have seen has worn off.

-You wait, man. Just let me up!

Michael couldn't be stopped, so I did not waste my time in trying. From where I sat on the floor, I had a full view of what the "naked" window revealed. The full moon was just above the horizon and it looked huge, as if God's hand had brought His beacon of light closer to us: not for us to examine, but for Him to examine our souls.

Shadows moved about outside. They were shadows that pressed against the glass pane leaving impressions upon the glass…the outline of a hand, a finger, a torso, but never a complete human form. The buildings and the street outside appeared distant as if the darkness not only robbed them of light, but of existence, as well.

Becky cried in Michael's arms.

Yvonne had fallen to her knees in prayer and supplication.

-What is going on? What has happened to us? Tell me, dearest Lord! Tell Yvonne!

A waste of good breath.

Melody knelt down by me and put her hand on my shoulder.

-Howard, let's get that lantern and the candles.

She helped me to my feet. We started toward the staircase.

Irene called out to us.

-Don't be too long. We'll be waiting for you.

Oshido went over to Yvonne and gave her comfort. Max and Sean were at the bar. Abraham was near no one at this moment. Rose stood closest to the window and reached out to touch the glass. I stopped her.

-Rose, I wouldn't if I were you. I have a feeling that it might shatter. And, after all, it is the final barrier between us and them.

Rose withdrew her hand and gave me a dirty look. She held grudges.

Melody and I climbed the stairs. I led the way to my bedroom. I flicked open the light switch, but the light was dim and depressing so I switched if off.

-The lantern is in the closet, on the door attached to a hook. The candles are in this top drawer.

Before I could move to get them, Melody put her arms around my shoulders and kissed me. I grew hard and passionate. I put my leg behind her knee and tripped her and myself down on to the bed. With one hand, I opened my trousers's fly and pulled my rod out.

-Taste it, first!

I sat just above her chest, not touching it for fear that my weight might hurt her. Her lips and tongue were moist and the inside of her mouth felt humid and damp as some of her lipstick rubbed off on my shaft. The pleasure was exquisite. I reached back to lift up her dress and grab her. I pulled my rod out of her mouth and already I was dripping.

I slid down to enter her. It went in smoothly and with no guidance. I pounded and drove it in, until I could no longer hold out. She stroked my sweaty back as I came and shot into that beautiful, tight hole.

I pulled out and got off her. Leaning against the bureau, I let my rod relax before pulling up my trousers. Melody walked over to the bureau, but did not come over to me. Her purpose was to fix her mussed up hair and retouch her make-up.

-Howard, turn the light switch on, please?

I did as I was asked. Her strawberry blonde hair was soon restored to its feathery texture. She reached into her handbag and touched up her lipstick. I smiled at the thought that my rod might still have some traces of lipstick on it.

Melody was ready. She opened the top draw and found the ten candles and took them out. I went into the closet and unhooked the lantern. She joined me at the doorway and this time it was she who switched off the light.

-Ready?

-Howard, I feel that you may leave us tonight. Come back to us or-

-"Or" what?

-Change something. And, if you do so, find me. Don't forget me.

-How can I leave you, Melody?

-There are ways. Here, I'll leave you my scent.

Melody reached into her purse and withdrew a small spray bottle. Before I could stop her, she squirted my neck with the perfume.

-Why did you do that? I don't want to smell like a woman.

-You won't. But, in a way, I'll be near you with every breath.

-Melody, I must ask you a question. Why do you ignore Sean? I thought you were his friend.

-I'm not his friend. I barely know him. I don't even like him.

-But, you steal documents for him.

-I haven't stolen any documents, Howard. I would never do that. Did Sean tell you this?

-Yes.

-He's a liar.

CHAPTER FIVE
THE SEANCE

-I'D LIKE to know what in hell they're doing up there.

-My dear sister...Rose, you know perfectly well what they're "doing" up there. Let's not pretend to be naive. And, I for one do not care.

-Ha! You're full of shit, Irene.

-Only if it affects the seance do I care. I won't stand for that.

-And, that reminds me, dear sister, of a little question I've been meaning to ask you. Why are we having this little seance of yours in the first place? You haven't filled us in on that, yet. You think it's gonna' help us any?

Irene hesitated before answering her sister.

-The answer to our difficulties lies outside the physical realm. No one here can give me all the answers that we need to survive this night.

-Including yourself, Irene?

-Yes, Rose. Including myself. I am not above the fray.

-Who in hell are we contacting anyway? Do you know that much?

-A woman whose shadow I saw on the staircase this morning. I could be wrong, but I think she's from that year 1947.

-Well, I hope this "shadow" knows what the hell is going on.

Max and Yvonne were exchanging comments.

-I wish they'd hurry up with that lantern. It's bloody dark in here.

-Yes, Max, I too am terribly frightened. Perhaps, another drink would help to calm me?

-Yvonne, you've had enough, I'd daresay.

-I've had enough of Howard and his games, that's for sure. He likes to insult people. He's cruel.

-I think Howard means well.

-I don't. But, Max, what do you make of all this? I feel that we are contemporaries and that I can speak freely with you.

-If I didn't know any better, I'd say we were all in some bloody nightmare. The trouble is: nobody is waking up.

-I think it is far worse than that. I know what my Aunt Madeline would say.

-What would the dear lady say?

-That all of us have been eliminated from an evil world that we did not fit into.

-And, who in God's name did this "eliminating?"

-At first, Max, I suspected Howard. But, I sense that he is as frightened as the rest of us despite his bravura and his bullying. He tries to hide it, but I can see through the bastard.

-So, who's your next suspect?

-Abraham.

Max's attention was distracted by Becky.

-Oh, Michael, I'm scared. I wish we could begin just to get it over with.

-I know, Becky. They'll be down soon enough. Are you gonna' be okay?

-I don't know. I guess I will. But, it's the strangest feeling because for the first time in my life, I actually feel like I'm with friends. I've always been afraid of people because they seem to know that I'm different from them.

-I know what you mean.

-Once, when I was taking the subway, these people who were sitting across from me, they kind of nodded to each other. And, I'm sure it was about me. I got off at the next stop. I couldn't stay on that train another minute. The look in their eyes was so mean and cruel. Michael, why were they looking at me like that? And, it wasn't the first time either.

-Just put it out of your mind. Like you said, you're with friends now. No one here is gonna' hurt you.

-They waste too much precious time.

Oshido, who was standing near the window, agreed.

-Abraham is correct. It is close to midnight and we must begin at once. Sean, help me place the largest of these tables in the center of the room. Then, we will place the chairs about the table. Quickly! Time is of the essence or we may be-

-Doomed?

-Yes, Sean. I was about to use that exact word.

Sean and Max carried and placed the round table in the center of the room. Each person brought a chair to the table. Rose wanted to put the drapes back up, but Irene stopped her. No. They must be seen by the moon and exposed by her light.

Everyone sat down and waited for our return. Melody and I joined them. I placed the lantern above our heads, dangling over the table: the lantern of light that would take the place of the sun. It would symbolize the warmth and serenity of His radiant light and balance the evil of the moon that was closing in upon us.

Melody sat to my right and Irene sat to my left. Sean was next to Irene and Michael sat next to Sean and, then, came Becky and Abraham who was now directly across from me. What fucking irony! Yvonne was to Abraham's left and, then, came Max, Rose, and Oshido who was on Melody's right hand side.

Irene struggled to speak in a calm voice.

-No one must speak once the seance begins. We must use our psychic abilities in our concentration. The circle must not be broken or else we will fail. And, I don't think we'll be getting a second chance. Now, place both hands on the table and touch fingertips.

Irene took a deep breath and began the seance.

-The woman whose shadow I saw today...come to us now and speak to us. Tell us who you are and what you know of all this. Save us! Save us from this evil! Speak through your chosen channel.

The lantern began to sway back and forth casting its light upon one side of the room and then the other side: brightness on one side and then darkness on the other side...day and night...life and death. No one in the bar knew where to look.

The moon was beginning to sink below the horizon. The room grew colder and darker until it was illuminated only by the lantern and the eerie light of the moon. Outside, the voices had stopped.

-Look!

Irene nodded in the direction of Abraham: behind him, a grey shadow moved. This shadow moved through the table...it moved behind Becky and stopped. It descended into the girl's body and took possession of her. Just a moment before the lantern shone upon Becky, the shadow had taken the form of a young, Latin woman. The woman spoke to us.

-Of course, I may now speak. The body is strange, but it's usable. Has no one here anything to ask me? I would have many questions if I were in your place.

Irene asked the first question.

-Who are you?

-A very simple question to answer. But, perhaps, I chose not to answer it, eh? What then? Tell me what would you then do? But, I'll answer it because it will benefit me as well as yourselves. My name is Yolanda Estravades. You see? It means nothing to you. I knew that it wouldn't.

-Are you the woman whose shadow I saw on the staircase?

-Pitiful, no? Reduced to a mere shadow; but, now I have substance, however imperfect.

Irene pushed on with her questions.

-Why a mere shadow, Yolanda? Why haven't you passed on?

-Because of him. Don't ask me his name, for I cannot say it. It should never be said.

-Why did you come to us?

-You need me to tell you what has happened. Can no one stop that lantern? I find it annoying. A sun should be stationary and not moving back and forth.

-What has happened to us, Yolanda?

-Ask the Hasid your question. He told you before. I'll tell it to you so that you can understand and there will be no mistaking my words.

Yvonne shouted at the now possessed Becky.

-Are we dead? At least tell us that much.

-Don't interrupt me! Death is the least of your concerns. You've all slipped through to that which is always present but cannot be seen. You find yourselves now on the other side of existence. It is the evil side of the glyph.

Irene continued to question.

-How and why did we get here?

-All of you possess psychic gifts which you'll have need of. None of you actually slept last night, am I not right? But, for a moment, you did "slip off." It was then that he pushed you through the doorway, as I was pushed through. Or, perhaps, you are the outcasts…the survivors of the end or their descendants?

Yvonne spoke the question that we all wanted to ask.

-How do we get out? Tell us that much.

-By never being here. No. I don't taunt you with riddles. What happened must be changed for all of our sakes and for the world that you thought you knew. Someone here will have to change the course of the world's destiny. You must prevent the cataclysm from happening.

Yvonne continued, but her voice betrayed her growing frustration and fear.

-Prevent *what* from happening?

-I can't speak of it. It changed the world. It was evil and perverse and horrible.

Irene took over the questioning, again.

-How can we stop this thing from occurring, Yolanda? For heaven's sake, how?

-One of you can slip back into the past. I'll help. Then, we must wait until we no longer exist in this phantasmic world.

-Why were you pushed in?

-As it always is, Irene, I knew too much. I knew him all too well. I knew of the event that would take place.

Again, Yvonne interjected, but without asking a question.

-Mon Dieu!

-Yes. Call upon Him for you'll need His help. His Son helps you now or all would be lost.

In a frightened voice, Irene asked her final question.

-Who is to "slip" through to the past?

-The moon...look...it sinks below a horizon which doesn't exist.

Max spoke up.

-Can you tell us more of this event? I'm not clear on that at all.

-It was the day the world ended.

Yvonne was close to hysterics as she screamed out.

-What? What is it that you say? But, we are alive, so how can this be? You're lying to us.

-I am not lying. Look at the moon. It sets.

An arm reached out toward the swaying lantern and knocked it down. We were plunged into darkness. Screams were heard and there was one scream of torture.

-It stopped.

-What stopped, Yvonne?

-Those horrible screams, Oshido.

Oshido addressed the others at the table.

-Is everyone present?

-Ha! Who in hell can see anything? It's worse than being blind. Irene? Are you there?

-Yes, Rose, but-

-I am here, but Becky is not. Her chair is empty. I am Abraham.

Irene spoke up.

-Howard's gone. I didn't feel him get up. He is gone, isn't he, Melody?

-Yes. But, I can still feel his fingertip.

-How interesting, dear. But, where is he?

-I'm getting up. Melody, where are the candles?

-We left them on the bar on the left hand edge, Max. Be careful.

Sean volunteered to help.

-I'll help you, Max.

The two men groped their way toward the bar.

-What the hell is this?

-Rose dear, are you all right? Please, try not to panic.

-There's something wet and sticky on this table, Irene. It's spreading!

-Rose dear, what in the world- Oh! Something is on the table.

Irene pushed her chair back, but not quickly enough to prevent the liquid from spilling on to her dress. Michael pulled away. Abraham pulled away, also, as did Melody, Rose, and Oshido, but all too late. All of them were stained.

Melody called out to Max and Sean.

-Guys? Please, hurry! Something's happening over here.

-Irene, it feels like blood!

-Dear Rose, please don't start a panic. I'm sure-

Michael shouted.

-Oh, my God! It is blood!

Irene's hand slipped on to the table and she screamed The lantern was once again lit. It was still dangling from its hook, but something or some bits of fiber obscured its light. One could almost see through these bits dangling long and loose like remnants of a spider's web.

Melody turned to look over her shoulder and saw a point of light coming toward her.

-Max, thank goodness. Someone's turned on the lantern.

Everyone at the table got up and moved back toward the bar. Another point of light appeared: this one nearer the table. It was Sean and he also backed away. For a moment, the blood stopped at the edge of the table and, then, in a cascade of slow motion, it overflowed. All nine people were back at the bar bumping into stools and pressing themselves against each other. More candles were lit by Sean and now each person held a candle: nine points of light in the darkness.

Irene knew what had to be said.

-Look at the lantern.

Yvonne screamed and could not be stopped.

-Mon Dieu! There she is- how did she- Ah!

The pale outline of a face permeated through the lantern's light like a long lamp shade with the outline of dead features. Murdered. Butchered. It was a part of what remained of Becky. The other pieces of her torn and mutilated body had been nailed to the ceiling above the table with the lake of blood beneath it.

Michael collapsed to the floor.

Max couldn't look away. He spoke to no one in particular.

-Skinned alive like some animal! Horrible! Horrible!

Oshido was aware that he could not blink his eyes shut. He spoke without taking a breath.

-She has been skinned alive like a slaughtered pig: cleanly and neatly and the rest of her is torn to pieces.

-Thanks for the run-down, pal.

-I state the obvious, Sean.

Michael wiped the tears from his eyes.

-Why Becky? Why did he do it?

-Howard didn't do this, Michael. I'm sure of that. He wouldn't do such a thing.

Yvonne stopped her screaming and addressed Melody with a couple of sarcastic questions.

-Oh? And, how do you know this, Melody? Where is your precious lover gone to? Eh? Answer us that, if you can. You can't.

-I can, Yvonne. He was pushed back through time to when this all began. Howard will help us. I know he will. He'll attempt to stop a terrible event from occurring, and that will bring us back to where we should be.

Sean looked at Melody.

-You hope.

Yvonne spat on the floor.

-Riddles! Riddles! How I grow tired of these damned riddles. I need a drink. Someone get me a drink!

-How will we know if Howie-boy succeeds?

-In all likelihood, dear Rose, we'll never know. We won't have any memory of this dreadful night, which is fine by me, dear sister.

Oshido spoke a warning.

-There is still a murderer amongst us. He is the cause of all this.

Sean laughed at nothing in particular.

-That puts me in a tight spot. I hope these candles have a long life to them.

-You interrupted me, Sean.

-Sorry, Oshido. Keep talking, man.

-Our murderer did not kill Becky so much as silence Yolanda.

-Hey, Oshido, man, have you noticed that there's no more noise outside? The hell voices stopped and those shadow figures are gone and it feels kind of warmer in here.

-Yes, Sean, I have noticed. As soon as the moon set-

Sean shoved his candle in Abraham's face.

-Hey, Abraham, what have you got to say? You've been awfully quiet, man. You're not holding out on us, are you?

-There are nine of us left. And, the light is once again natural. The candles dispel some of the darkness. Whatever you do, do not let them go out. And, look outside. The street lamps are lit and I see lights on in the building across the street. Perhaps, we should investigate?

-I'd hold off on that for awhile, pal. The lights may be back on, but I don't see anyone walking around.

Rose spoke and couldn't take her eyes off the window.

-I'd have to agree with Sean on that one, Abraham. We'd better stick together for now. Who knows what the hell is out there.

-But, there is a murderer in this bar. I shouldn't stay here.

-No one should stay here, Abraham, pal. And, you can leave any old time you feel like it. No one's stopping you. I'm not. Just don't expect any company or help.

-You don't like me, do you, Sean? You feel as Howard did.

-Maybe. You may just be right about that, Abraham.

-Poor Becky.

-Right! You sound real broken up about it, Irene.

-Don't be impertinent, Sean.

Oshido addressed the group.

-We must be patient and pray for our friend to succeed. To kill Becky was easy for our murderer; but, perhaps, Howard will prove more difficult to stop.

Sean laughed.

-Start rooting for Howard. And, that murderer might still be here with us.

PART TWO: EDWARD

CHAPTER SIX
YOLANDA

THE SPOTLIGHT blinded me. I tried to lift my head up, but couldn't. I felt the cold seep through my buttocks as it caught the direct route to my insides. I tried to turn my head, but the thought of moving was painful. I saw another arc of light from the corner of my right eye and, then, a shadow of a figure jumped across me. This shadow narrowly missed me and caused ice chips to splash on to my face. For just a moment, there was silence and, then, the sound of blades scraped the ice.

-Are you crazy? Do you want to kill us both? How did you get there and who let you into the rink? If the custodian did it, I'll see to it that he's fired. Why don't you answer me?

When I didn't respond, a note of concern crept into her voice. It was a Spanish woman. A beautiful Spanish woman.

-Are you unable to get up? I can see that you're having difficulty. I'll call the custodian over.

-No. Don't do that. I'm all right now.

I got to my feet as this beautiful woman watched. I slipped and caught myself by putting out an arm to brace my fall. She laughed and put her hand under my elbow.

-Slipping, no? Let me help you. We'd better get you off this ice or you'll slip, again, for sure. Come on, let Yolanda help you.

We walked to the chairs just outside the rink. Yolanda sat next to me, still with her hand on my elbow. I looked down at myself and saw some of what I was wearing: a trench-coat, wing-tip shoes, and slacks.

Yolanda looked at me and smiled.

-Now, you must answer my questions. Whom am I speaking to?

-I don't think that I know.

-Oh? Are you unwell? Take out your wallet and that should tell us something.

I reached into my suit jacket and took out the wallet. Yolanda took it from me and looked through it.

-I like your name. It's a strong and masculine name.

She was pleased with the amount of money in the wallet, as well.

-Tell me my name, please?

-Edward Mendez. And, you're a private investigator, Mr. Mendez. I like that. Are you investigating me? Have I done something wrong that I don't know of?

-I don't know. I don't think so.

-I'll give you back your wallet now. I suppose if you don't remember your name, you don't know how you got in here either?

-I don't. Where exactly am I?

-You're in my private ice skating rink.

-You own this place?

-No. But, I do rent it on an exclusive basis.

-What for?

-I'm a figure skater. I'm practicing for the next National Championships. Today, I was trying not to break a leg and land a double-axel.

-You didn't break a leg. Did you land that double-axel, whatever that is?

-Almost. I was about to attempt another one, when I almost fell over you.

-Where is this rink?

-In New York City, of course.

-And, what year is this…the exact date?

-It's March 31, 1947, of course. You don't know this?

-I don't or I wouldn't ask.

-You don't seem certain about what you don't know. I'm almost done here, so why don't we go for a drink? I'll change. Stay here, I won't be long.

I stared at the ice rink, but that wasn't on my mind. I lifted my left hand and stared at my finger. It felt like someone's finger were pressing against it. I ran my fingers through my hair which was short and slicked back. I closed my eyes and tried to get myself oriented but without too much success.

1947.

An ice rink.

An occupation, but no identity.

Christ!

I kept staring up at the clock above the exit door.

-I'm ready to go. Are you asleep, Mr. Mendez?

Yolanda was a beauty: dark hair that cascaded to her shoulders, almond shaped eyes and full, sensual lips. Her skin was flawless and her hands were ready to caress every part of a man. I was pretty sure of this.

-You might as well call me Edward. Why don't you take me to your favorite place?

-I know of a good pub close by and, of course, I couldn't go there by myself.

The ice skater took me by the arm and flirted with me.

-Thanks for helping me out like this.

-I see no reason not to help you. I'm hungry and you'll escort me to dinner. I find you quite appealing, Edward.

The walk to the pub was only a few blocks. It was cold and windy and the sun was on the point of setting. It cast long shadows as we crossed the street. And, it was so funny…it was as if I could see the two of us from outside of my body: two figures in the oncoming dusk.

-Stop here for a second.

-Why, Edward? I'm cold and it's starting to get dark.

-You're wearing a coat. You won't freeze. And, besides, you're an ice skater so you should be used to a certain amount of cold.

-Why are we stopping here?

-There are people walking by. I like that. Look at the sun. It's gorgeous. It should never have to set. It's a thing of such ultimate beauty: a red ball of light against that beautiful blue sky.

I was close to tears.

-It is a beautiful sunset. You like beauty, Edward? That's nice in a man. You're sensitive.

-It's late March, you say?

-Yes. The last day. Now, let's go in, please.

We entered the pub. Yolanda led us to a corner table in the crowded and smoke-filled room.

-Good. I like this table and the owner keeps it reserved for me.

-You know the owner?

-Yes. Not that well, and not the way that you think.

-I wasn't thinking of anything.

The place was crowded. According to Yolanda, it was a popular place for college students to drink beer, smoke, and discuss philosophy. Yolanda and I took off our coats and waited to be served. It didn't take long before the coffees were brought over. She asked me for a cigarette. I reached into my inside jacket pocket and took out a half-used pack of Lucky Strikes. I offered her one and reached into my pocket for a match.

Yolanda smiled at me and drew on her cigarette.

-I needed that. But, are you not smoking, Edward?

I lit up and this seemed to please her. I sipped at the hot coffee which tasted good and took a deep drag on my cigarette.

-Now, do you remember anything about yourself and how you came to be flat on your back in the middle of my ice rink? I don't understand how I didn't see you walk in.

-I don't have any answers for you. It's as if my life were beginning on borrowed time.

-Oh? On whose borrowed time? How interesting. I'm also interested in such things. I have friends-

-What about yourself? You must be wealthy to be renting an ice rink. Are your parents supporting you?

-Quite frankly, it's none of your affair as to how I support myself. But, I'll say this to you: I know the right people and I know how to get on their good side.

I took another drag on my cigarette and exhaled the smoke away from Yolanda.

-Uh-huh. Are your friends interesting?

The young woman laughed at this.

-They think so. Sometimes, they can be. Perhaps, they'll be here tonight? They often come here for drinks and dinner.

-Tell me about them. Will I like them?

-Well, there's Marlena who is quite ugly and on the fat side. But, she's fun and clever. I like hating her.

-Who else?

-Others. Dolores might be here later. Yes. I think she'll be here tonight.

We drew on our cigarettes. I offered Yolanda another one. She refused.

-One is enough. I really shouldn't be smoking at all. It's not good for a figure skater.

-It's probably not the best habit in the world.

-So, Edward, where do you plan on spending the night?

-I haven't looked in my wallet just yet. Did you happen to see an address in it?

-Yes. But, it's quite a distance, you know.

-Where?

-Staten Island. I've never been there. So, why don't you spend the night with me? You might have trouble finding your way back to your place.

-Thank you. I think I'll take you up on that. Do you have an extra towel for me?

-Of course, but unfortunately, no pajamas.

-We'll manage without them.

With the tip of her finger, Yolanda traced a valentine on my palm. Her touch was sensual.

-You have masculine hands and you're tall. I like tall men. Are you selfish in bed, my sweet? I like that. I like to be played rough with, but not too hard for pain must be quick and sweet and savored.

-I'll try to remember all that.

-Look! Here come Marlena and Dolores: an odd pair, no? Don't worry, we'll get rid of them quickly enough. Dolores will know enough to go, but Marlena might not. She's the pushy type.

Dolores, although not quite as beautiful as Yolanda, was still a beauty in her own right. Marlena, on the other hand, was stout and disheveled. Her shoulder length, salt-and-pepper hair was an uneven mess that had seen better days. Underneath her trench-coat, she wore a housedress.

The two of them sat down without being asked. Dolores sized me up. Marlena openly stared, but good-naturedly. She was pretty direct with her questions.

-Well, Yolanda, new boyfriend?

-Yes, Marlena. I just happened to meet him at the ice rink. Edward Mendez, please meet my good friends Marlena Lake and Dolores Sarney.

-Miss Lake? Miss Sarney? Pleased to meet you both.

-Well, Yolanda, your new boyfriend looks interesting and intelligent. I like him. I'll get straight to the point.

-Do you ever miss it, Marlena?

That was Dolores who spoke with a cattiness in her voice.

-Never. But, sometimes you do, lady. Now, shut up.

-Don't speak to me like that. Who do you think you're talking to? your son?

-Watch it, lady. Never mention my son's name. Never.

Yolanda interrupted this argument.

-Marlena, you were about to say something?

-Yes. Anyway, Edward, we belong to this…shall I say, encampment? Are you familiar with the term?

-Yes. I think so.

-You do know something. Good. Meet us here tomorrow night with Yolanda and we'll talk further: make it early, say around five o'clock? You can get off from work, can't you? You see, Edward, we need another man with us.

-For what, Miss Lake?

Marlena played with the glass ashtray and then remembered to ask for a cigarette.

-Edward, in a manner of speaking, I'm in the research business and I need to procure certain rare documents. Time is of the essence. Anyway, I must be going now and Dolores will come with me. I don't mean to be abrupt, but I've an appointment to keep and it's imperative that I not be late. Dolores, let's go.

-Oh? Giving orders to me? I'm not your slave.

Marlena snapped at this.

-Such a bourgeois term; but, remember, my dear, you'll do as you're told or else.

Dolores's eyes glared with hate; but, she kept silent.

Yolanda looked at her friend in sympathy, but she was glad that they were leaving. Marlena gulped down her coffee and asked me for a couple of cigarettes. Yolanda smiled and shook her head. Dolores followed Marlena out, but she turned around to look at me and Yolanda.

-What was that all about?

-Girl talk. Nothing to concern yourself with. Let's order some food and, then, we can go back to my place. Of course, you'll order for me.

-I was going to.

-I don't like to take any chances. Although, I'm taking one now, perhaps.

-Let's eat. We'll talk about our "chances" later.

The food was good and the portions generous. I noticed that Yolanda wasn't a big eater. She was content to pick at her food and sip her Jack Daniels.

I drank my scotch and soda and chain-smoked.

-Come back to bed, Edward. I miss you.

-I will, baby. Just give me a couple of seconds.

I was in Yolanda's bathroom and stood there naked with a semi-erection. And, for the life of me, I couldn't stop staring into her bathroom mirror. My face was clean shaven. My dark hair was cut shorter at the sides than at the top and my dark, brown eyes had an almost vacant look in them. It was my face. It had to be. I ran my hands along my naked body: firm and well-defined. My thoughts seemed new: well tempered, even-keeled and patiently awaiting questions and answers, but to what? The cold, tiled floor felt good against my bare feet. Every touch and every sense that I could feel felt so good.

My erection was complete. I wanted to have more sex with Yolanda…to please her and caress and burrow into that loveliness that so needed my attention. I got into bed with this beautiful creature, carefully slipping my rod in, but not too hard and not too fast.

-Mmm…my lovely Edward that feels so good. Now, talk to me and ask me anything.

-Who are you, baby?

-Me? Such a strange question to ask. What exactly do you want to know?

-Just who are you- uh! You're real moist. I'll go easy.

-Mmm…nice. I come from Spain- from Barcelona and my family migrated here just before the war. I have quite a large family, but I keep in contact with almost none of them. Why should I?

-I don't know. Are you a professional figure skater?

-Of course not. I'm an amateur. I'm preparing to enter the competitions beginning next year. I'm almost ready for them.

-So, your parents aren't supporting you?

-You got that out of me; that was clever of you. No wonder you're a private investigator. I appreciate cleverness in people. But, I'll beat you to the next question: I have a sponsor who believes in my talents and that's how I can afford to practice in the rink as often as I do.

-Is this sponsor a lover?

-I don't have to answer all of your questions.

-Oh, God! Hold still…*hold still, baby!*

I came, but stayed on top of her, holding her and never wanting to pull out of that wet pussy.

-Edward? You're crushing me.

-Sorry. That any better?

-Much better.

-Tell me about your friends, Yolanda. And, thank you.

-Oh? Which ones? Marlena or Dolores. Dolores is prettier and a little interesting, but Marlena is much more interesting and, in her strange way, talented. I like talented people, so I keep her as a friend.

I pulled my rod out and Yolanda handed me some tissues to wipe myself with.

-Tell me more about Marlena. You sure don't miss her when she walks into a room.

-Marlena is strange and powerful. I must use that word: "powerful." But, I'm not really sure that I'm able to describe her power to you.

-Try.

-She's superstitious and this makes her act very strange at times.

Yolanda changed the subject.

-Are you hungry? Go and help yourself to some food in the kitchen. I've plenty of cold-cuts and there's even a loaf of Italian bread. Make yourself a big sandwich so that I may pick from it without angering you. Do you want a robe, my love?

-No. It feels good being naked.

-Good. I prefer you that way, too.

I walked into the small, white kitchen and opened the refrigerator which was packed with food. The sight of it all made me hungry. But, I stuck to the makings of a large, hero sandwich and some wine.

-Yolanda?

-I'm still here waiting for you.

-Keep talking to me.

-Marlena runs an interesting business.

-Document research, she said?

-That's how she chooses to phrase it.

I walked back into the bedroom with the food and wine on a serving tray. The wine glasses, I held in my other hand

-Mmm…yummy. I'll pick at your sandwich.

-How would you phrase Marlena's line of work?

-She's in the blackmailing business, sort of. She collects documents and things and even people. Dolores is a part of her collection. I don't know why Dolores allowed herself to be, but who can speak for other people's motives?

-Is Marlena blackmailing Dolores?

-I don't know. I guess that she must be.

-Don't you and Dolores share things?

-Maybe I do know and maybe I just can't tell you, Edward. I won't betray a trust.

-Fair enough. Dolores has got herself a pretty decent friend. Let's get back to Marlena.

-Yes?

I got up for a moment to go and look out the window. Yolanda's place was in a corner building right near an intersection. Automobiles passed by often and people were still walking on the sidewalks. I noticed one man by the bus stop waiting for his transport to arrive. I walked back to the bed and plopped myself down. Was I asking too many questions?

-Tell me more about Marlena's blackmailing business.

-I don't really like to talk about it. I don't know if I should say anymore to you.

-Trust me.

-Should I? I don't know if I should. It could be unwise for me to be too trusting.

-Think of my confidence as an investment: one day, you might want to draw from your Edward account.

-I like how you put that. I'll take the risk, but it gives me the creeps to talk about it in detail. Marlena is smart and resourceful and maybe more resourceful than anything else. But, I don't understand her or why she robs things.

-To blackmail, you have to steal.

-The blackmail is only a part of it. She's doing something else. It's something that she's obsessed about. And, she does bad things, too…evil things that she knows I disapprove of.

I got up, again, to look out the window.

-Why do you keep getting up for, Edward? You know, someone might see your beautiful, naked body. Come back to Yolanda, for I have need of you so much more than the world. Let me caress you.

-Hmm.

-What is it? What do you see?

-A man who I thought was waiting for a bus.

-I haven't heard any buses go by. Maybe, he's still waiting for one.

-Maybe.

I got back into bed and took a big bite of the hero sandwich while Yolanda poured the wine.

-There, Edward, a bus. He's gone now.

-What does Marlena do that you disapprove of? You don't seem to disapprove of her blackmailing business, or at least not that end of it.

-I neither approve nor disapprove. People are blackmailed every day, so I can't concern myself with that. No. That doesn't disturb me. Marlena robs other things besides the documents.

-Like what?

-Her targets are places that you would never dream of robbing or searching for documents in. She robs from churches and synagogues and probably other holy places, as well. I don't know how she selects them; but, I'm sure it's with a purpose in mind.

-What does she steal from churches and synagogues? That's a pretty strange combination.

-Is it? Maybe not. Marlena steals holy vestments and the sacred objects on the altar.

-What does she do with them? She can't possibly sell them.

-I don't think so. Some of them she keeps and others she discards. And, the church documents, I imagine, are for blackmail, no?

-It depends on the documents: personal files *could* be used for blackmail. But, I'm not sure what kind of documents are kept in a church that would constitute a blackmailing scheme.

-Dolores says that she doesn't steal many documents: only a few, and most of those she ends up burning.

-What about the sacred objects? Does she perform holy rituals with them?

-You make me laugh, Edward.

Yolanda drank her wine and nudged me to do the same. I did and took another bite of my sandwich.

-She performs no rituals and forget about holy ones. There's nothing holy about Marlena. Dolores says that she's afraid of something.

-Who?

-No, my sweet, not "who," for Marlena is afraid of no one: not any man or woman. Forget it. But, she's afraid of something. I see it myself. Each day, she becomes more and more frantic and superstitious.

-I'd like to know what she's afraid of. She doesn't look like the sensitive type.

I got up to go to the window, again. Why did I keep doing this? The sublime movement of a man with a beautiful woman to watch him? Maybe. The cold air felt exquisite and decadent against my genitals. I sat on the window sill and looked out on to the intersection not caring if anyone saw me. The window sill felt cold. That man still waited for his bus. It was the same man. And, I knew that he wanted to look up.

-Yolanda? I think I'll send our friend on his way. He's still loitering out there. I don't like his looks.

-No! I will.

Yolanda gathered up her robe from the floor and hurried over to the window. She wasted no time in flinging it open.

-You! You out there! What do you want? Go away or I'll send my boyfriend down to beat you up.

I leaned out the window, pressing against Yolanda. I shouted down to the bastard.

-You heard the lady, pal. Beat it!

The man ran off down the street. His clothing was strange: a long, black great-coat and some type of bowler hat.

Yolanda pulled me back into the room and got her arms around me.

-Good to have a man. Now, come back to bed and comfort Yolanda.

I pushed her back down on to the bed and stayed on top of her. Not too hard.

-Now, baby, why do you think Marlena is frightened?

-I don't *care* why. Ask her when you see her tomorrow night. Maybe, she'll confide in a man.

-She lives alone? What's so damned funny?

-Marlena is never alone. She's surrounded by people all the time. Her children-

-Hold up.

-Oh? Going too fast for you, Mr. Private Investigator? You ask an awful lot of questions, but I guess that's part of your profession. Make love to me, again, please.

-How many children does she have? Is there a husband to go along with this family portrait? I'd sure like to meet him.

-She has two children: Gabriel and Susan. Susan is nice but plain looking; but, she's smart and clever. I like her because she's nice. And, there is no husband. It wouldn't surprise me if she had him killed or did the deed herself. They say that he died of neglect. A good way to kill someone, no?

-And, Gabriel?

-I don't think that he'll ever marry. I don't like him.

I opened Yolanda's robe and put my hand on her lovely pussy to warm myself.

-What makes you say that? Doesn't he like girls?

-I've no idea. I don't really care. You know, Edward, you don't have to come tomorrow night if you don't want to.

-I'll be there. If for no other reason, it's something to do.

-Marlena will take us all back to her place. She's a good hostess who doesn't hover over her guests all the time. She'll probably take you aside at one point in the evening.

-Tell me some more about yourself.

-I bore myself.

-Somehow, I think you're vital to all of this.

-You speak in riddles, you know that? I don't know what you're talking about. What am I vital to? I'll bet that you can't even tell me that, can you?

-I can't, baby. Wish I could. But, how the hell did I get into your ice skating rink tonight? Maybe…just maybe, I was headed there.

-I don't know. That was strange. I told you that I didn't see you come in, that's for sure.

-Maybe Marlena can tell us.

-Maybe. Edward, you smell nice. It's almost a feminine scent, but on you it's quite delicious and appealing.

-So, you won't tell me more about yourself? Give.

-No. But, I'll make a bargain with you: when you remember your past, I'll come to you with my past.

-Deal.

CHAPTER SEVEN
EVIL MEN

YOLANDA MADE me breakfast that morning. It was only seven o'clock, but we both wanted to get an early start.

-I like cooking for a man and waiting on him and pleasing him.

-Sit on my lap for a minute.

I kissed her and looked into her eyes and grew hard. Her hair was pulled back into a soft and silky ponytail fastened by a diamond clip.

-What day is today?

-Friday, darling Edward. Where will you be going? You may keep me company while I practice, you know. We can even go back to bed for a little while longer, if you like.

-I'll drop by later. I think that I'll pay my own address a visit first and see if I can scrub off any memories.

-You live on Staten Island, so it will take you the better part of the day. Do you know your way there?

-I seem to. I think.

-Don't get lost…come back to Yolanda. I'll be waiting for you at the ice rink, and try to be there at five, please.

-I will. But-

-What is it? Do you remember something of your past?

-No. But, I've been thinking about how I came to be on that slab of ice at that particular time.

-And?

-You didn't see me come into the building, did you? If I'd walked on to the ice, I'd have fallen or at least slipped.

-It's possible that I didn't notice you. When I'm practicing, I'm pretty focused on what I'm doing. But, maybe, you did fall on the ice and hurt yourself.

-Makes no sense. Somehow, I was *placed* on that ice to meet you.

-Who put you there? Do you know?

-Interesting how you phrased that question. I don't know "who" put me there, but…

-Say it.

-I think I know why. It was to meet you and your friends.

-Why?

-Somehow, you're a key component to all of this.

-To all of what?

-That's the question that just maybe your friend, Marlena, can answer.

-Don't trust her, Edward. I don't. And, she's nobody's friend.

-I'll remember that, baby. Better get dressed now.

I showered and got dressed. I needed to go back to my place for a change of clothes and a shave: having the tiny stubble on my face bothered me. I felt sloppy.

Yolanda told me what bus to get for the ferry, and now I was waiting at that bus stop. It was the same bus stop that that man had been at last night.

Yolanda walked back into the kitchen and cleaned up. She placed everything on the sink rack to dry, except for one cup and saucer. Another cup of coffee was necessary and, perhaps, that would erase her sudden feeling of disquiet.

She placed the cup of coffee on to a tray and brought it into the living room. Yolanda enjoyed eating a late breakfast by herself when everyone else was scattering off to the work place and the like. She sat down and sipped the hot coffee. It was an excellent brew and not too strong.

The phone rang.

Yolanda almost dropped the coffee cup to the floor.

The phone rang, again.

Yolanda answered it.

-Yes? Who is this?

-You know perfectly well who this is. I have not called to identify myself.

-What do you want of me?

-You sound frightened. Have you done anything that you would prefer I not know of?

-Why do you ask me such a question? I've done nothing.

-Liar. But, we will address your lies on another occasion. I have called to give you instructions. Listen carefully for I will not repeat myself. Keep your new boyfriend close to you.

-I have no boyfriend.

-Keep Edward Mendez close to you. I trust that you are capable of that. Introduce him to Marlena's circle of cronies. I look forward to having two enemies. I find it stimulating.

-Marlena is your enemy?

-An excellent question. Yes. We are enemies.

-Does Marlena know this?

-She is an intelligent woman who is capable and sharp. One day, I'll have to kill her.

-I don't want to hear this.

-You needn't be told anything further for now.

-Who is Edward? Can you tell me that much?

-Another question, Yolanda? And of all the people to ask it! If you could only appreciate the sheer irony of your question. Edward Mendez is a man whom Marlena has had the intelligence and good sense to try and recruit into her fold. He is not a follower, for he has the determination of his soul.

-He doesn't even know who he is.

-An identity is as useless an encumbrance as a name. Edward Mendez literally feels his life and knows his purpose. He searches for the answer to the question: "to what end?"

-What's that question? What's Marlena so afraid of?

-Your association with me has raised your intelligence. You have improved yourself, Yolanda. However, I will not directly answer your question. Marlena also feels the pulse beat of her life. Years ago, I allowed myself to tell her of a coming event in a cryptic form, of course. I laid out a few pieces of the puzzle for her. She has now spent the better part of her miserable life trying to connect the pieces and fill in the missing portions: a daunting task even for her.

-What's this coming event- no. Don't tell me! I don't want to know. It must be terrible.

-For a moment the scales will meet and heaven and hell will merge.

-What are you saying to me?

-It is difficult to explain to a mortal.

-What do you mean by that? Who are you?

The receiver clicked on the other end of the line.

It felt good to be aboard the boat and alone with my thoughts. The vista was endless and the arc of the sky disappeared over an infinite horizon. The water was choppy and the boat was rocking back and forth. With one hand, I held on to the railing and with my other, I held my container of coffee.

Staten Island loomed large and bleak. Why the hell would I have picked such a place to live? I shook my head in bewilderment at that thought. Maybe when I reached my place, I'd have an answer to that question.

People started coming out of the boat's cabin and headed toward the accordion gate. I looked around and saw no one I recognized which wasn't the biggest surprise. I finished my coffee, tossed the container into a garbage can, and took out a cigarette from the nearly empty pack. In a few minutes, the boat docked. I was one of the few people getting off.

I asked for directions at the ticket booth. I bought my ticket and boarded the train. Several passengers were aboard so I wasn't riding alone. I tried to take a look at my fellow passengers: businessmen. They sat close together, but didn't speak to each other: dark suits huddled together and not even a whisper shared amongst them.

I felt like reading a newspaper so I looked around for a stray one that someone might have left behind. I should have bought one at the terminal.

The ride seemed tedious but, at last, the train pulled into my stop. The doors opened and then closed and the train pulled out. I heard movements from behind and jerked my head around. The businessmen had gotten off the train and followed me along the station platform. One of them tossed his newspaper into the trash. It was on this pretext that I stopped and turned about in order to get the paper. I stole a glance at them. The brims of their hats were turned down so that you could scarcely see their faces.

I picked up the newspaper and followed them off the platform and down the steps. They turned right and vanished. I hurried down the stairs and almost lost my balance. When I reached the sidewalk, I looked in both directions, but they were gone. I stared about at the desolate landscape: trees that were barren and gnawed by the winter's onslaught and the grey and dead silence of the air. For all I knew, I had stepped into another world that had never known life. There was nothing left to do but to try and find my way.

I walked fast and with purpose allowing my gut instinct to carry me along. At the fourth block, there were a few stores with apartments on top of them. I took out my wallet and looked at the address printed on one of my business cards: Edward Mendez/New Dorp Lane/Staten Island, New York/Private Investigator. My business card had a Manhattan address on it, as well: 423 John St./Room 1007 and a Manhattan phone number. I should have gone there. Later. After I'd finished here, I'd go and take a look at my office.

I found the address and went to a wooden door. It was locked. I took out my keys and fitted one of them in and the luck-of-the-draw was with me as it clicked open. I walked in and slammed the door shut behind me. There were no lights on the stairway. I took the steps two at a time and noticed that the staircase was narrow and rickety.

At the top of the stairs, there was another door to be unlocked. I took my keys out and, once again, luck was with me. The door clicked open and a telephone began to ring: my telephone. I groped for the light switch, flipped it on, and started looking around. The room was small and looked as if it had recently been painted. The only furniture was a twin bed, a bureau with a mirror, and a night stand. The phone was on the night stand right next to the neatly made up bed. I grabbed a hold of the receiver.

-Edward Mendez here.

My name had a nice sound to it. Yolanda had been right about that. I fumbled in my pocket for a cigarette and glanced into the mirror. I needed a shave.

-Mr. Mendez? You don't know me.

It was a woman's voice with a German accent.

-You're right. So, tell me your name.

-My name is Rosamund Spender. I was given your phone number by Marlena Lake. Of course, you know who I am speaking of.

-I don't think that there could be another one like her. She makes a pretty strong first impression.

-Yes. That is true. Miss Lake is an extraordinary woman.

-What can I do for you, Miss Spender? How did you know where to reach me?

-Marlena gave me your phone number. I told you this, so why do you ask, again?

-I felt like it. How did Marlena come by it?

-I would imagine, since you apparently did not give it to her yourself, she looked it up in the telephone directory. Is that so strange?

-Not at all. She doesn't waste any time.

-How odd that you should say that, Mr. Mendez. You are quite right in that time is sacred to Miss Lake. But, now I must get to the point of our conversation.

I lit up and took a deep drag on my cigarette. For a moment, I heard the sound of a piano playing, but I couldn't place where it was coming from.

-Marlena wants you to come directly to her place and to bring Yolanda with you.

-Why the change of plans?

-Miss Lake will have food for you when you arrive. I am only guessing now; but, I am certain that she has much to discuss with you that could not be said freely in a public place.

-Are you a friend of Marlena's?

-I am not a part of her group: that is what you meant to ask, wasn't it?

-You could say that.

-I know Miss Lake only for a short time. I am not sure that I like her. I do like her daughter, Susan. I do not care for her son. I cannot say that to her, but to you, I may say it.

I sat down on the edge of the bed and continued to smoke. Interesting that she and Yolanda had similar feelings about Marlena's offspring. From my vantage point, I could see South Beach and what must be the ocean. Some memory in the back of my mind was echoing a warning…a warning about a house? I lost the thread of the thought.

-And, now, I will answer you another, as yet, unasked question, Mr. Mendez.

I looked around for an ashtray.

-And, what's that, Miss Spender?

-How I come to know Miss Lake; am I correct?

-Keep talking.

-We met in Germany. It was right after the war when things were quite ugly and still are. She came to me, Mr. Mendez. I did not look for her because I had no reason to. I didn't even know that Marlena Lake existed.

I unbuttoned my top collar and loosened my tie. I was to learn that that statement wasn't entirely true.

-Marlena sought you out in Germany, Miss Spender? How come?

-Yes.

-What did you have that Marlena wanted?

-Your questions are deceptively simple. You are clever.

-You haven't answered my question so maybe I'm not so clever.

-First, Mr. Mendez, you must promise me something.

-I don't make promises.

-Smart man. I am returning to Germany tomorrow morning.

-Why, Miss Spender? Should I care?

-I will tell you why, which brings us back to your question of a moment ago. You see, I have recently lost my sister.

I took a drag on what remained of my cigarette. For a moment, my heart stopped beating.

-I'm sorry to hear that, Miss Spender. What was your sister's name?

-Her name was Valerie. She was beautiful. And, I can sense that you are affected by this. Do not try to deny it.

-I wouldn't. It's as if I feel the pain of Valerie's death and the actual sound of her passing away.

I did feel the sting of death…the onrushing of another dream and existence on to a new landscape of visions.

-You would have loved her. She was a student of the piano and her talent was exceptional. I can still hear her playing. It was an evil god who took her from us.

-It was your sister, Valerie, who Marlena was looking for; is that it, Miss Spender? Did I get it right?

-Yes.

-Do you want to tell me why? If you don't, that's all right. I respect your grief.

-I thank you for that; but, I can feel that you already love my sister. So, I will tell you some of it.

I lit another cigarette. The room's light faded as I put another question to Miss Spender.

-Did Marlena meet your sister?

-No. Miss Lake arrived too late.

-What was it that Marlena wanted?

-My sister was an innocent. She was sensitive to other presences and felt things intuitively. I am not doing Valerie justice.

-You're doing just fine. Did Marlena want Valerie's advice?

-No. She sought Valerie's knowledge and got what she wanted.

-How's that? Did your sister keep a journal?

-You know more than you pretend, Mr. Mendez. My sister kept quite an extensive journal and, of course, she confided in me.

-Have *you* confided in Marlena or don't you trust her enough?

-I have given her the journal. However, I still keep my sister's confidence.

-I'm thinking, Miss Spender, of your sister and about her dreams. Don't ask me why.

-Why do you not surprise me? Miss Lake has selected a worthy new friend.

I got up from my bed. I felt a cold current of air waft over me in what had up until that moment been a cozy and warm apartment.

-Mr. Mendez? Are you still there?

-Yes.

I walked over to the window, picked up the phone and balanced the receiver on my shoulder. I pushed up a few slats of the venetian blinds and saw those same businessmen pass just beneath the window. They must have finished their business and were heading back to the train station. Impulse told me to follow them, but common sense told me that I was outnumbered.

-Mr. Mendez?

-There are four men walking down the street, just outside my window. I have this impulse to follow them. Should I?

-Do not! Tell me what these men look like: businessmen, no? That is, until you look into their faces.

-Yes..

This woman's fear was contagious. I had a bad case of the "willies" just then.

-Stay where you are and do not allow them to see you. I know of these men and so does Miss Lake.

-That doesn't surprise me.

-You take to joking on something most dangerous. These men were involved in Valerie's death. They would have killed me, as well, if they had had the opportunity. And, an attempt was made on Miss Lake's life shortly after Valerie was murdered.

-I think I'll head back into the city. Maybe, we can meet for coffee and discuss-

-No. I cannot meet you until tonight. I've much to do before I leave for Germany tomorrow morning. And, I want you to stay in your rooms for another half an hour, at least, or until you are certain those men have gone. Promise me that.

-I promise.

-Good. And, now, I must go. Goodbye.

-Hold up. What's Marlena's address?

-Yolanda knows where to go. Good day.

I put the phone back on the night stand. I stood there stock still, trying to take in that phone call. If I'd had second thoughts about going to Marlena's tonight, those thoughts were gone. It bothered me that I had to rely on a stranger for help. But, help for what? I could just walk away from all this, try and get my memory back, and go on with my life with Yolanda, of course. Was that really an option? I didn't think it was. If just to satisfy my curiosity, I wanted to find out what I was about to become involved in. That conversation just now with Miss Spender had intrigued the hell out of me and so had those four men. Yep. I was going to see this through.

I walked over to the bureau and looked at myself in the mirror. I still had on my trench coat. I took it off and flung it on to the bed. I opened the top bureau drawer and went through the clothes...my clothes. I picked out a dark blue shirt and matching tie, but something caught my attention. Just underneath the shirts and ties, there was a gun which looked like an old German hand pistol: a Walther P38 Semi Automatic. Interesting how that fact just clicked into my consciousness. I picked it up and opened the casing; it'd been fired, but not recently. In the same bureau drawer was a shoulder holster; the kind that goes across the chest. I put it on over the blue shirt and tucked the Walther into it. Better. Now, I felt a lot better. Maybe, I'd been a WWII vet. and this hand pistol was a souvenir. No. This gun was a part of my occupation. I'd used it as a civilian. I knew this had to be true.

I opened up the other bureau drawers and in the bottom one there was a carefully folded dark green leather jacket. Nice. I put it on and it was a perfect fit, just about concealing the gun underneath. Now, I could protect myself and Yolanda. Amazing what a gun can do for a man.

My office was right on the corner of John St. and Broadway. It was within walking distance of the ferry: about a half of a mile or so. The building was a ten story brownstone. When I walked into the lobby, I had to look at the directory even though I knew the floor number. The elevator man spotted me. I didn't like his look.

-Forget your floor, Mr. Mendez?

-Just looking over my neighbors. Goes with the profession.

-Going up?

-You guessed it. Tenth floor.

The ride up was slow. I could see that the elevator man was sizing me up. He wasn't being discreet about it. He must have sensed something different about my demeanor. I pretended not to notice. I didn't want to risk engaging him in conversation where he would have had me at a disadvantage.

The elevator car stopped with a slight jerk. He turned to look at me. I didn't like this guy or his arrogant manner.

-Tenth floor, Mr. Mendez.

-Thanks.

-Dan's the name. Don't you remember? You feeling all right, Mr. Mendez. You look kind of preoccupied.

-I'm just bad at names. Thanks, Dan.

I walked straight down the hall with my footsteps muffled by the carpeted floor. My office was straight ahead: Edward Mendez: Private Investigator was stenciled on to the frosted glass. I took out my three brass keys and selected the one that I hadn't used yet. I opened the door and glanced back. Yes. Dan, the elevator man, was staring after me. I waved to the bastard, went inside, and closed the door behind me.

-Man! What the hell was his problem? And, that look on his face...was it one of pure contempt? I think it was. I'd better keep an eye out for him.

I walked past the small, wooden desk and looked out the window. I scanned the horizon and then looked down on to the street below. Cars were moving southward along Broadway and pedestrians were rushing back to work from their lunch hour. The AT&T building was right across the street. And, was that Dan going into the building? It was. The bastard was up to something, but I had no time to waste on him now. I wanted to look through my files before heading back uptown to pick up Yolanda.

I turned to face the file cabinet which was right behind my desk and to my immediate left.

I was organized. Good. I liked that.

I started rifling through the files: manilla folders that were kept in alphabetical order. There were case files on clients: divorces, separations, suspected extramarital affairs, some local break-ins. Nothing earth shattering, that was for sure. And, none of it was familiar. Not even the slightest disturbance of a subconscious memory.

I glanced over to my left. The old wooden desk, which was my desk, was clear of any papers; only the green blotter was there with a glass ashtray in the right hand corner. No photographs. No mementos. I guess I wasn't the sentimental type.

I was now at the bottom drawer of the file cabinet and about to call it quits when a folder marked World War II Artifacts caught my interest. I pulled it out and sat down with it at my desk. I opened it up. Inside were newspaper clippings of the bombings of Hiroshima and Nagasaki and a list of names. Now, I was getting somewhere: people who I could look up and investigate about…what? Christ!

The names on the list were: Ramona Chen, Werner Hoffmann, Sr. and Werner Hoffmann, Jr., a father and son most likely, Nella Mendez, Dorothy Mendez, Victoria Mendez, and Catrina Mendez. Were these four ladies my relatives? Must be. But, why were their names listed in this file with regard to World War II? Intriguing. And, there was one last name: Marlena Lake. Why wasn't I surprised?

I copied each name. Yes. It was my handwriting, all right…well, my print. With the exception of Marlena, I couldn't place any of these people, not even the

four ladies who shared my surname. I took out a cigarette from the fresh pack that I'd just bought at the
newsstand outside and lit up.

Names on a piece of paper.

Newspaper clippings of two devastated cities.

And there were some black and white photographs
of an actual atomic blast. It started with a photo of the
initial drop made by the bi-plane and went right up to
the mushroom cloud spiraling upward toward the atmosphere. In this last photo, there was a small white
speck and a "fold" in the upper left hand corner? A flaw
in the lens? Over exposed film? I opened the top middle
drawer and found what I was looking for: a magnifying
glass. I examined this last photo with the lens. No. I still
couldn't make out the object or the reason for the
"fold," but the more I looked at it, I could feel my blood
turn cold.

I put away the magnifying glass and shoved the
photos back into the folder. There was no time to think
about any of this. It would have to wait. Some inner
voice "told" me, though, that one day, if I lived long
enough, I'd have to face some new horror connected to
these names and photographs.

I'd lost track of the time. It was just past four-thirty.
I was riding the Uptown Lexington Avenue Express.
Where the hell had the time gone? The uptown bus
would've been too slow and I didn't want to keep
Yolanda waiting. For some strange reason, I had taken
out those Atomic Bomb photos from my file again to

have a second look at them. My "eye" had kept focusing on that last photo with the "fold" in it. I wish to hell I'd had the actual negative which might have told me something. On the back of the photo, there had been a handwritten name: Ortiz and the stamp of the actual photographer: Maxwell. Two more names to look up. I was warming up to my job as a private investigator.

I was riding in the middle car and standing up. I had a newspaper folded under my arm and was holding on to one of the leather straps. I was wearing my leather gloves. It was funny how I'd found them in my apartment. The weather was getting colder outside and I just automatically reached into the drawer of the night table and took out the gloves. Maybe, if I put myself on "automatic," my past would come back to me.

The subway car was crowded with evening commuters. I'd gotten on at Chambers St. and had just made it on to the train as the doors were closing. I'd gotten a seat, but had given up my seat to an attractive young woman. I didn't have the time to start up a conversation with her, so I unfolded my newspaper and scanned some of the headlines. Russia was pushing forward with its atomic bomb testing. So much for a once trusted ally.

The train was zooming past Astor Place when i glanced over to my left. In the next car down, I spotted him: Dan. Now what the hell was he doing on this train? As if I had to ask!

I let go of the leather strap and pushed my way through my fellow passengers. I reached the connecting door and yanked it open. He saw me and took off down the car. I stepped over the gap between the cars and pulled open that connecting door. I now had one hand on my gun. I released the safety catch. Without apology, I shoved my way through the crowd. The bastard had a head start on me and he was a smaller man who could more easily weave his way through the commuters.

The train was slowing down on pulling into Fourteenth St. I moved to my right to get a look out the door. The platform was jam-packed with people. Was that him getting out? I think it must have been. He ran up the downtown stairwell and got lost in the crowd. I decided to stay on the train. If I ran into this character again, I'd have a few questions for him. I put the safety catch back on the gun.

CHAPTER EIGHT
A WARNING

DOLORES WATCHED Yolanda skate. The young girl admired her friend's athletic ability and dedication. She called out to her.

-I still haven't seen you do a double-axel jump. You'll have to, you know, if you want to stand any chance of winning the Nationals. Are you afraid to try it without your coach here?

Yolanda ignored Dolores's remark and did a double toe-loop jump. It was well executed with good height and momentum and the landing was well placed.

-That wasn't a double-axel. I know the difference, even if you think that I don't.

Yolanda did her front extension with her right leg and this brought her to the edge of the rink and face-to-face with Dolores. She was breathing heavier than she wanted to.

-Is that all you know how to do is to criticize? I know what I have to do. I don't need you to tell me. And, besides, that was a double-toe loop.

-Where is your coach today?

-Fridays are his days off, so I do as I please and perfect the jumps I know that I can do.

-I was only teasing you. Don't you know me by now?

-Too well. Hand me that towel, please. I don't want to stop too long. I'm starting to sweat.

-Sweating is very unbecoming to a woman, but I love it on a man, no?

-Oh, yes...very much so.

-Did Edward sweat last night?

-Yes. In all of his right spots, too.

Both women laughed as Yolanda dabbed at her forehead.

-He was lovely and hard and strong and the hurt that he caused was sweet.

-Yes. Your jumps are high today.

-Thank you.

-And, what of your other friend?

-I have few male friends.

-I should be insulted that you take me for such a fool. I know that you're avoiding my question.

-I know who you mean. What do I care? I don't.

-You should, Yolanda. He pays for everything. I wouldn't want you to lose him.

-You want him? Maybe, I'll give him to you.

-How brave you are today. Tell me, has Edward given you such strength?

-Maybe and maybe not.

-I think he has. I like him; but, can he afford to keep you? What are his prospects?

-He has money, but how much I don't yet know. He's a private investigator.

-Are you serious? That's pretty risky, no?

-Yes. But, it can be profitable, too, with the right clients.

-And, what about your other-

-I don't want to speak of him. He's unimportant.

-I don't believe that.

-Oh?

-You're too easy for him.

-And, just what do you mean by that?

-He calls and you're there, always. He must have spies on you, Yolanda. And, what would he say about Edward?

-That's none of his business.

-He wouldn't agree with you and you know it.

-I have to skate. Talk to me. I can hear you from the ice.

Yolanda glided toward the center of the rink as Dolores watched. She did some of her straight-line skating that she knew would be required of her to compete. It might bore her friend, but she needed to work on it. She skated the entire length of the rink on both

sides and kept careful watch on her form and extension. Not bad. Not there just yet, but not bad.

-Well, Dolores, nothing to say? I thought that you wanted to talk and keep me company? No answer?

On impulse, she skated to the center of the rink and readied herself for a double-axel jump. She looked over her shoulder and began the momentum forward. She positioned her body for the circular movement and, in particular, her right leg that she would use to lift herself off the ice. Yolanda got ready to make the leap. The time and the moment and the position were right: lift-off, two and a half rotations. She landed it successfully. However, her leg came around a little too soon and this forced her to touch the ice with her hand. The jump, it-self, had been a good one. If she could pull it off in the artistic program, she'd be hard to beat.

-There! Did you see that? A little unsteady at the end, I admit, but still not so bad. Dolores? Cat got you tongue? No criticism this time?

Yolanda looked at the spot where her friend should be, but all the chairs were empty.

-Are you hiding? Where are you?

Yolanda resisted the urge to skate over to the chairs. She felt cold. She folded her arms about her torso.

-Dolores, answer me and stop playing this game. I don't like it.

Yolanda's light, blue costume made her feel ex-posed and vulnerable. She wanted to rush to her dress-ing room and throw her coat on and flee from the skating rink. But, to do that, she would have to leave the ice. She knew that on the ice she was safe, and it was she who held the advantage. The ice beneath her feet was a shield of protection and even a weapon.

The young ice skater stayed close to the center of the rink. She looked around the dark arena. The lights had been dimmed and even the overhead arc lights weren't as bright as they should have been.

-Dolores?

She whispered her friend's name. The lighting dimmed even more and, then, there was a sound…a vibration. Yolanda could bear it no longer.

-Dolores! Answer me! Please! What you're doing is cruel.

The lights went out altogether and Yolanda was left in almost complete darkness. The tiny, dirty windows near the ceiling were her only source of light. She stared at the dim light and even this light was giving way to darkness.

-No!

Were those snowflakes Yolanda saw falling against the windows? She heard a loud thunder clap. The young woman started and almost fell down on to the ice. She put her arm out and stopped her fall. She heard a rumbling of thunder. The snow turned to rain and beat against the small window panes.

She raised herself back to her feet and glided toward the chairs where Dolores had been. She had to go this way in order to get to the dressing room. She tightened her muscles and made ready to either bolt to the imagined safety of the dressing room or skate back into the middle of the ice rink.

The frightened ice skater went to the edge of the rink and reached for her skates' safety guards. She picked one up, and a hand grabbed her wrist. She screamed and fell to the ground.

-Yolanda. It's Edward.

-Thank God you're here, Edward. Pick me up and hold me.

-What's wrong, baby?

-No. Don't put me down just yet. Hold me in your arms. When did you get here?

-About a minute ago. Why are all the lights out? I can't see a damned thing.

-Let me down. Dolores is gone. I don't know where. She just vanished.

-Maybe, she just got bored and left.

-Without telling me? No. She would never do that. And, besides, she was coming with us to Marlena's. Something's happened to her. Help me to my dressing room. I don't want to stay here.

I picked Yolanda up, again, and carried her to the dressing room, knocking over several wooden chairs on the way. I got to the door and kicked it open. It was pitch black inside.

-Here.

I placed her into a chair that I could just barely make out.

-Edward, I have some candles in that drawer, but I have no matches.

-Use mine.

There were two candles in the drawer: I took them out and lit one.

-Yolanda? Get changed and let's get the hell out of this death trap.

It didn't take her long to change into her street clothes, but putting on her make-up was another matter. I didn't rush her because it did her mind good and eased her, somewhat. I heard the rain pounding against the roof. The thunder was unsettling, but the gun I had on me helped soothe my nerves.

-Okay? Let's get moving.

-I'm ready.

She checked the contents of her purse. I picked up her gym bag.

-Edward? We should look for Dolores- oh!

The vibration of that thunder could be felt. Did I imagine it, or were the walls shaking?

-We'll look for her on our way out. Let's move.

I took her by the arm and lead her out into the stands. Why there was only one way into and out of this place made no sense. There was practically no light in the place and even the ice radiated blackness. The only light that came in was through the tiny windows when the lightning struck.

We treaded our way through the wooden, collapsible chairs, some of which had been knocked over by me.

-Will we be safe outside?

-I think we're almost there. And, it's better than staying in here. At least outside we'll have some running space and more light.

Lightning struck and this time Yolanda cried out, but not in fear.

-Over there, Edward! I saw someone. It was moving like some kind of animal.

I took my gun out. I whispered to Yolanda.

-I saw it, too.

A dark figure had opened the door and slid out...yes..."slid out" into the night. It didn't look quite human, but what else could it be? My hand tightened its grip on the gun.

-Come on. Let's get out of this death trap.

-Edward, I'm afraid. He may be out there waiting for us.

-I don't think so. If he had any brains, he would have confronted us in the dark or stayed hidden.

Lightning struck, again.

-Look! Dolores! Is that you I see? Dolores?

We saw the outline of a girl on a chair through the flashes of lightning. We approached the figure as if we were in a sort of a trance. We couldn't focus or sustain our vision. Yolanda made the sign of the cross several times. I extended my arm toward the girl in the chair. I spoke to her.

-Dolores? Is that you? Answer me.

The girl moved as the thunder vibrated the building. It turned toward us.

-Is she alive, Edward?

It was a corpse that moved…a corpse that had been disemboweled. There was a gaping hole through her body where one could see the back of the chair. And, yet, her glazed eyes stared at us.

It spoke.

-He did this.

The body collapsed to the floor. Yolanda became hysterical. I couldn't have calmed her down even if I had made the attempt. Instead, I pushed her toward the exit. When we reached it, I kicked it open and we found ourselves in the pouring rain. In a matter of seconds, we were drenched. I saw a movement in the shadows, got out my gun, and took a shot at it. Man, that felt *good!* It ran off, but I think I hit it.

-Mother of my Savior! I didn't know you carried a gun on you.

Yolanda screamed and her eyes went wild. I slapped her hard across the face to bring her back. I had to raise my voice to get her to listen.

-Get a grip! We have to call the cops and tell them what's happened.

-No! Not the police! They won't help and there's nothing they can do except to make trouble for us. And, that gun, how will you explain it?

-A murder's been committed.

-A murder? Is that what you call it? I can almost laugh at that word! No. It wasn't a murder. It was a ritual slaughter. It was a warning for me! I know this.

-Come on. Let's head for that restaurant that you took me to last night. I need a drink…maybe a few.

-No. We must go to Marlena's place. She'll know what to do and we should be safe there.

-That will put us in her debt; is that what you want, baby?

-We're all in someone's debt; does it matter so much to whom?

-Touché. But, I still don't like it.

-Edward, please, I can't stand it anymore.

-All right, you win. Let's hail a taxi. Christ! I'm soaked to the damned skin!

-We can change at Marlena's. A taxi won't be necessary. We can use Dolores's car. I have an extra set of keys on me.

We crossed the street. I followed her at a half run to a parked car. She threw the car keys to me.

-Here, Edward, you drive. I'm too nervous. I'll tell you where to go and just keep your gun handy.

I noticed that she checked the back seat before getting in; this girl wasn't taking any chances. We got in the car and locked the doors.

Yolanda grabbed me by the shoulder.

-And, now, dear Edward, drive like a madman to Marlena's and pray that no one has seen us.

-You okay?

-No. I'm cold and upset.

-Here. Move closer to me. Reach into my jacket pocket for my cigarettes, will you?

-Got them. Nice jacket. You look good in it.

-Light one for me, baby? Glad you like the jacket.

Yolanda handed me the lit cigarette. I took a deep and grateful drag on it. Just what I needed. I noticed that the rain was coming down harder than it was a few minutes ago. Even with the windshield wipers working, I still had to strain to see the traffic up ahead.

-When you get to 89th St, turn right until you reach 1st Ave. Edward? Why were you so late? I was beginning to worry.

-Sorry about that, baby, but I stopped off at my office downtown.

-Oh? And did you find out anything about yourself?

-It didn't trigger any memories, if that's what you mean.

-So, why did you stay so long?

-I got sidetracked looking at some photos.

-You going to tell me what these photos were? There must have been a lot of them for you to look at.

-No. Only a few.

-So, tell me what they were.

-They were photographs of an atomic bomb blast.

-What?

-A sequence of photos ending in the mushroom cloud and-

-And? You were going to say something.

-In that last photo, baby, there was a white...speck? I guess that's what you'd call it. I'm not too sure.

-Probably a flaw in the film, no?

-That's what I thought.

-But? What do you think now.

-There was this sort of "fold" in that part of the photo.

-You mean the photograph was bent?

-No. The "fold" was a part of the actual photo. And, for some reason, Yolanda, it bothered the hell out of me. I kept staring at it, trying to make some sense out of it.

-Edward, that's interesting because I think I may know what that fold is.

-Give, baby. You're one up on me.

-I've always been interested in science, especially astronomy. Dolores and I went to this lecture at the "Y' a couple of years ago and a Professor Lange was outlining the dangers of atomic bomb testing. He said that the initial impact could have an effect on the earth's rotation. It could slow it down and that would cause the planet to move closer to the sun.

-Christ! What else did this Doctor Lange have to say?

-He mentioned his own theory about parallel times and shifts in the space and time continuum. I didn't understand some of the mathematics; but, he was concerned about "rips" in time caused by the intense heat and radiation into the atmosphere.

-What did he mean by that? And, by the way, you're impressing the hell out of me, baby.

-He said that the bomb blasts could be opening up portholes into anti-matter galaxies.

-So, that white speck was anti-matter?

-I don't know. He said that other civilization could use these portholes to come here.

-Assuming that there are other civilizations out there. And, that's a pretty big assumption, in my opinion.

-He seemed to think that they were more advanced than we are. He even talked about a parallel earth.

-Here's 89th St. I'll make the turn. We'll talk a lot more about this later. Right now, we've got a date with Miss Lake.

CHAPTER NINE
MARLENA

A YOUNG, blonde girl answered the door to the upper east-side townhouse. She was wearing pants and an open collared shirt. The masculine outfit suited her to the proverbial "T." Her blonde hair was pulled back in a ponytail.

I took an immediate liking to this girl. I wanted to hold her for her warmth and intelligence and her self-command which I was certain that she possessed. She didn't just stare at Yolanda and myself, she assessed us and the probable situation that we'd just come from. Her voice was clear and distinct and educated. The voice of reason.

-Please, come in and take your coats off. You're both drenched. Sorry for stating the obvious.

Yolanda smiled at the girl and introduced us.

-Susan, I want you to meet my new boyfriend, Mr. Edward Mendez. Edward? This is Susan, Marlena's daughter.

-Pleased to meet you, Mr. Mendez. Mother mentioned that you would be dropping by tonight, but she didn't say exactly when. Yolanda, where's Dolores? Is she trying to find a parking space in all this rain? It might take her awhile.

Neither Yolanda nor I could think of an appropriate answer. Susan saved us the trouble.

-No. She's not with you, is she? Please, come in. Why don't you slip out of your shoes and I'll bring you some towels? Better still, why don't I take you to separate bathrooms upstairs?

-Thank you, Susan. I know where they are and, of course, we'll both need robes.

-You can borrow one of mine. I'll get one for Mr. Mendez.

-Thank you, but-

-You can't stay in those wet clothes, Mr. Mendez. I'll let my mother know that you're here. She's pretty anxious to meet with you.

Susan walked through the parlor and into the dining area where I could see two people eating. Susan walked past them and into another room. I thought I heard her going down wooden plank steps. Right off the hallway was the parlor, and all I could make out was a round, oak table whose legs had been cut to shorten the table. There were cards on the table: strange, big cards with colorful images on them.

-Edward? Let's go and change before we catch our deaths of cold. You can look at the cards later.

Yolanda's look was not a nice one. She had caught me staring after Susan and said as much as we walked up the carpeted stairs.

-Susan is interesting, no? Do you like her?

I made no answer.

When we reached the first landing, my new girlfriend pointed toward a door.

-Go in there and get undressed. You can even take a quick shower. And, dear Edward, think of me naked in the next room and grow hard…for you see, I'll be thinking of you.

-I'll try real hard.

-Do more than just try. Now, go. I don't want you to catch a chill.

As soon as I got into the bathroom, I stripped naked and grabbed a towel and dried myself down. I forgot my erotic promise to Yolanda. I put my gun on the straw hamper; the nozzle was still warm.

I took another towel, draped it about my waist, and went to the mirror. I ran a comb through my damp hair and rubbed my teeth with my forefinger. And, then, my pinkie finger…my left pinkie finger felt so strange, there was still that pressure on it.

I stared into my eyes and saw a stranger staring back at me. He was handsome and young and had a soul that was fashioned similar to my own; but, his soul bore the mark of more experience even though his youth belied such a thought.

A knock on the door.

-Yes?

-It's Susan, Mr. Mendez. I'll leave the bathrobe on the doorknob and the slippers by the door. Take your time; but, there'll be fresh, hot coffee for you when you're ready to come down. Are you hungry? I'll put a couple of pot-pies in the oven, if you like. I'll see you downstairs.

-Susan? Thanks, again.

I heard her walk down the hall and knock on the other bathroom door. I opened the door and took the bathrobe and bent down for the slippers. I took off the towel and replaced it with the robe and carefully adjusted my gun underneath. Where I went, that baby was going with me. I slipped my bare feet into the black slippers that were just a little too big.

Patiently, I waited for Yolanda to emerge from her bathroom because I didn't want to walk downstairs by myself. Impatiently, I walked over to the door and knocked.

-Yes?

-Yolanda?

-Yes, Edward?

-Ready yet?

-Of course not. I'll be a few more minutes, so you may go down without me.

-Go down where?

-Into the dining area, of course. Don't be modest. Susan likes you and she'll put you at ease. Now, go downstairs and wait for me. I won't be too much longer.

I walked down the hall and took the stairs two at a time and found myself in the parlour. No one was there, and I saw that the strange cards had been neatly placed into three piles face down. I reached down and flicked one over: it was the Knight of Wands: a handsome, young man with fire in his hair. I resisted the urge to pocket this card because I didn't know why I would want such a strange souvenir whose symbology was lost on me. I took it, anyway. Slipping it into my pocket, I walked into the dining room where a young man and woman were seated at a table.

-Excuse me, I don't mean to interrupt.

-That is no problem.

The young man spoke with an accent that I couldn't place. He was young and had an arrogant look about him. The woman got up and extended her hand. She was thin with her hair pulled back in a tight braid. I took an immediate dislike to both of them, more so the woman.

-Good evening, Mr. Mendez. I recognize your voice. We spoke on the phone earlier today. I am Rosamund Spender and this is Erich Manfred who is an acquaintance of mine. He is accompanying me back to Germany.

I shook hands with Erich, but it was Rosamund who spoke to me.

-Won't you please sit down with us? I feel that we have much to talk about and very little time to really say anything. I am tired, Mr. Mendez, and soon must excuse myself for the evening.

I sat down and tried to make myself comfortable in one of the hard-backed chairs which wasn't an easy thing to do considering that I had nothing on underneath my bathrobe. I looked about the room and noticed that the furniture was old and bore the mark of a particular time period that I was unfamiliar with.

Erich stared at me; but, I ignored him.

-I'm sure that Susan will soon be out with your food, Mr. Mendez. Perhaps, I may offer you a cigarette? They're German cigarettes and strong.

-Thank you, Miss Spender.

I took one and Miss Spender lit it for me with the lighted candle from the center of the table. She placed the candle back in its holder and glanced at Erich.

-Erich, do you want one?

-No.

-I will get directly to the point: it concerns my dead sister, Valerie. I have given Miss Lake her journal, and I give you permission to read it, as well. Miss Lake is not to keep it from you. Perhaps, the two of you will be able to make some sense of her murder.

-I appreciate your trust, Miss Spender, but-

-There are no "buts," for I feel that doomsday is upon us all. My sister's life mattered, mine does not.

-I've got a few questions for you.

-I will try to answer them.

-You mentioned that Marlena had come to Germany seeking information.

-Yes. My sister was a concert pianist. In Germany, she was well known- that rain, it beats against the house so terribly!

-Is there a light switch? It's too damned dark in this place.

Erich laughed at my question.

-Marlena prefers candlelight: brings out the romantic in her!

-Miss Lake had read about my sister; but, it wasn't her skills on the piano that interested her. Valerie was an innocent- Erich, I will slap you if you continue to laugh!

Erich stoppet laughing.

Miss Spender continued.

-Valerie's powers of clairvoyance were also known to the public and that is what interested Miss Lake.

-I understand; but, Marlena never actually met Valerie.

A thunder clap filled the dark room; but, the candle's flame didn't even flicker.

-Yes. But, Miss Lake did make it to the funeral.

-How was Valerie murdered?

Erich leaned forward to stare even more intently at me.

-I will answer that one. The method of my girl-friend's death-

-"Girlfriend?"

-Yes. Valerie was murdered in a unique way: the thinnest of metal rods was driven through her heart. But, that was not the only unique feature of this crime.

The metal rod extended from the ceiling to the floor: it penetrated the bed. It took the police hours to remove it. Have I explained it well, Rosamund?

-In a cold-blooded way, Erich, you've done well.

-"Cold-blooded," you call me? Perhaps, you are right; but, the facts are cold-blooded.

I interrupted the two combatants.

-Miss Spender, I mentioned four men to you on the phone. You sounded pretty distressed about that.

It was Erich's turn to interrupt me.

-You have seen these four men, Mr. Mendez? Consider yourself lucky to be alive.

-Four men were seen leaving the scene of the crime after my sister's murder; and, there were four strange men that very afternoon who had failed in an attempt on her life.

-Who saw them?

Erich grinned as he answered me.

-An entire audience of people. None came forward. They were too busy saving their own necks.

-Was an Hasid seen there at any time?

Erich spat on the floor.

-None was mentioned. Why do you ask?

-A man was hanging about Yolanda's place last night. I thought that there might be a connection. I could be wrong.

The hate and revulsion poured through Erich's voice.

-I'm sure that you're *not* wrong. It wouldn't surprise me in the least. Yes, Mr. Mendez, I'm not ashamed of my beliefs.

Rosamund reached into her purse.

-Read my sister's diary and here…here is a photo of her. She was beautiful, no? And, why are you laughing, Erich?

-Oh, no reason. Perhaps, I am just nervous.

Thunder claps came and went and still the candle's flame didn't so much as flicker. I got up from the table and Erich motioned for me to sit down.

-I apologize for my rudeness. Please, sit down.

-I think I'll see what's keeping Susan. Excuse me?

I couldn't get out of that room fast enough. I walked into the kitchen and caught Susan in the act of placing two pot-pies on to a serving tray. The kitchen was spacious, but dark like all the other rooms in the house.

-Hello, Mr. Mendez. I was just about to come in and fetch you. Mother should be downstairs in the basement. Why don't you go downstairs, and I'll bring your food to you? Mother wants to speak to you and you'll find her interesting. And, you'll probably form a most definite opinion about her.

-I'll see you downstairs, then, Susan.

I nearly walked into the door, but caught myself just in time. I took the stairs two at a time and found myself standing in a finished basement of sorts. I say "of sorts" because it looked more like a spruced-up bomb shelter.

The door opened and Susan came down with the serving tray. I got out of her way, because I knew that she would refuse any offer of help. She placed the tray on the coffee table and poured some coffee for me.

-Sit down, Mr. Mendez. There's milk and sugar here for your coffee, if you like. I hope you enjoy the food. I haven't succeeded in poisoning anyone, yet.

Susan and I laughed. I walked over to the sofa, picked up the cup of coffee, and drank it. Man, that hit the spot!

-Good coffee. Thanks. Mind if I call you "Susan?"

-Of course not, Mr.-

-Edward.

-Edward. Mother should be here shortly; but you can't run a clock by her. We only have one clock in the house, as a matter of fact. I hate to leave you alone down here.

-Then, don't.

Susan didn't like my interrupting her.

-But, I'm drying your clothes out and I don't want them burnt to ashes.

-Won't you sit down for just a minute? I won't bite. Promise.

-I really can't. There are your clothes, and I'm in the middle of a research paper. I'll tell mother that you're waiting for her; assuming that I can find her. See you later.

Susan turned to leave and had one foot on the first step when she stopped short and started.

-Hello?

-What is it, Susan?

-I thought that I saw something in the window…a face, I think. I can't be certain.

I walked over to the window, which was at shoulder level, but all I could see was a branch blowing against the dirty glass pane. I ran my hand along the concrete sill. The walls were thick and the window was insulated with mesh wire.

-My mother's imagination must be rubbing off on me. I better watch myself or I might become as superstitious as she, which is not a logical way of looking at the world. See you later.

Susan walked up the steps and back into the kitchen. I walked over to the couch and drank some more coffee. I was beginning to relax and feel warm. The couch was comfortable enough so I kicked off my slippers and crossed my legs and even my feet felt warm. I loosened my bathrobe and, leaning over, picked up a pot-pie and tasted it. Not bad.

The storm raged on outside as the rain hit the house like sprays of bullets meant to murder the people within: interesting sound effect, but unnerving.

I rubbed my hand along my smooth chest and opened the bathrobe a little bit more…yes…I was in the mood for some sex. I thought of Yolanda and tried not to get an erection. Not easy.

The door opened and someone came down the stairs with a heavy footfall At first, I couldn't make out who it was because of the dim lighting. I had to wait for the figure to approach me.

It was Marlena. I tried not to smile at her appearance and demeanor. She wore a London Fog trench-coat and open-back house slippers. The trench-coat was opened and revealed a checkered housedress. Marlena's salt-and-pepper hair was pinned-up with a dozen or so bobby-pins. She held a pair of nylons in her hand and in her other hand was a hair brush. Her movements were feminine and almost coy. It was quite a sight.

-Good evening, Mr. Mendez. How are you on this perfectly dreadful night?

-Right now, I'm dry and warm. And, thanks to your daughter, Susan, I'm eating a pretty decent meal. She's a pretty good cook.

-So, I see. Oh, please don't bother to get up. And, you may call me Marlena.

Marlena sat down next to me on the couch and stared at my chest. I thought of Rosamund and Erich and I realized just how unfinished our conversation had been. I had the impulse now to run back upstairs and finish our discussion.

My hostess started unpinning her hair.

-You're looking very pensive, Edward. What are you thinking about?

-Right now? Rosamund and Erich. I can't quite make those two characters out. If I didn't know better, I'd say that they hated each other.

-Oh, yes, Valerie's sister and her Nazi friend. What were you discussing? Tell me.

-Our conversation kind of drifted off. It was my fault. I was hungry and went looking for Susan. I kind of walked out on them.

-I assume that you went hunting for food and not my daughter? She's a dear girl but, alas, plain and almost dowdy; wouldn't you say?

-No. I wouldn't. She has a charm and quick-wit. I like her. I didn't find her to be dowdy at all.

-She is quite intelligent: a genius, in fact. She's of great assistance to me in my work even though our philosophies are quite different. But, we were discussing your conversation with Rosamund and Erich. I can safely assume that you were discussing the murder of her sister, Valerie, and the dead girl's journal.

-Rosamund gave me permission to read it.

-Did she? It is in my possession now, Edward, and I give you *my* permission to read it.

-But, Marlena-

-Rosamund is a fool. I will never allow her to have her sister's journal back. I've had to tolerate both her and her Nazi companion for the past few days. However, tomorrow they leave for Munich and good riddance to them both.

My hostess had almost all the pins out of her hair which fell past her shoulders and into a disheveled mess. She looked over at the window as she addressed me.

-What time is it, Edward? I never wear a watch as they make me nervous. They don't define time, but merely regulate and restrict our perception of that un-definable phenomenon. Don't you agree?

-Just past seven o'clock.

-Good. I expect to be up all night and that will give us sufficient time to discuss matters.

-That's why I'm here.

-I do have so much to tell you and even more to ask of you.

-Have you spoken to Yolanda? She may have something pretty extraordinary to tell you. Dolores has been murdered.

-Everything has been taken care of. You were quite right not to inform the police about it. My son, Gabriel, is disposing of the body as we speak.

-Marlena? I'm really at sea here. What is this all about? What the hell's going on? I can't even phrase the damned question.

By this time, she had all the pins out of her hair and began combing the mess.

-I always feel like Cleopatra when I'm doing this. Do you think that I look like her? You know, Edward, she was actually rather funny looking?

I didn't know how to react to that question. It seemed like a contradiction of terms. Marlena smiled and combed her too long hair. She sank further back into the couch. She saved me the trouble of answering.

-Now, as to your question which is my question, as well. Shall I state it for you? Perhaps, then, we can work our way from the beginning and pool our information?

Again, I was saved the trouble of answering.

-I have terrible circulation and that's why I'm so pale. Do you feel sorry for me, Edward?

Marlena put her nylons on my lap.

-Do you mind? I'll lose them, otherwise.

I smiled at this strange woman and at the rain and at the darkness. And, I felt like an idiot.

-And, now, the question: when will the event occur?

I was lifted out of my body. I saw a circle of people suspended in the night and a beautiful woman with the most extraordinary aquamarine eyes was sitting next to me.

-Edward?

-What?

-For a moment, it seemed that you had left your body.

-I did. I was in a strange place with people I didn't recognize. It might have even been the inside of a bar and grill. I don't know. But, Marlena, what about the event?

-I feel that it will occur soon...sometime this month. It will mean the end of the world.

I took a deep breath.

-I think you'd better tell me everything, if you can.

I slipped my bare feet back into the warm slippers. Outside, the thunder and lightning had stopped, but the rain continued to come down.

-The tale becomes even more bizarre. I must start from the beginning: a beginning that will end with your reading of Valerie Spender's journal. Sit back and relax and do take your slippers off.

Marlena flipped her hair back and began her story.

-The year was 1922 and, at that time, I was a young and proud woman. However, in my own way, I was naive and, as you've guessed, rather curious about things that matter to life and death. I was as poor as the proverbial church mouse and not properly educated. I came from a large family, all of them uneducated and rather vulgar, except for myself, of course.

Another contradiction in terms?

-I was the daughter of poor immigrants, if you can imagine such a thing. We lived in a poor section of the city, and I faced constant ridicule from all quarters. None would dare to ridicule me now, Edward. None.

She continued with her narrative.

-I had to work for a living; but, I managed to visit places: churches, synagogues, and temples and the like. I sought for things that would make my life better and give some sort of meaning to my mundane existence. And, you might say that I found what I was looking for. Of course, as is always the case, it was to be in a perverted form.

-I don't get you. What were you looking for?

-You will. I would arise early every morning, so as to make the utmost of otherwise wasted time. I would read from the Bible or the Zohar or even Blavatsky's books. I read at fever pitch and I learned what I still didn't understand...the beauty and the art of discipline. These were my hours removed from the world and I cherish them still.

-I'm listening.

-It was during these early morning retreats that I learned of a certain Judaic practice: the early morning prayer at synagogue. To my astonishment, women were permitted entrance into even the most Orthodox sanctuaries; separated as they were from the men. Still, I attended and, then, one Saturday, Edward, I strolled down to the Battery and met him.

-Yes? You're not going to stop there?

-But, my story precedes itself. I must go back and explain everything to you. I attended synagogue with the hope of also finding a husband: a good, Jewish man who would provide for me, so that I could educate myself further. However, that was only a secondary consideration: my main objective was knowledge...the hidden knowledge.

-The occult.

-It has always fascinated me from the time I picked up a Bible. And, then, one morning, I met him. It was after a crowded and uncomfortable service at the synagogue. I was sitting there amongst these people and I could feel his presence. I felt his eyes upon me; but, I couldn't actually see him. I stayed longer than I normally would have...and still I couldn't see him. I knew that he hadn't left, not yet and not without me.

Marlena paused and took a deep breath.

-After nearly everyone had left, I was forced to leave, finishing the pitiful sustenance that they give you and listening to their ceaseless banter. As a stranger, I knew more of their religion than they did. I had taught myself Hebrew. I studied the Holy Qaballah: the sacred glyph. Are you familiar with it, Edward?

I drank my coffee and nodded for her to continue

-That day — and, perhaps, you'll answer my question later — I took a long and leisurely stroll down to the Battery. At the time I was reading Madame Blavatsky. I looked for an empty bench. I chose one closest to the water's edge. Before I could even open the book, a man sat down close to me. I was annoyed, as I wanted privacy. Edward, my lover was sitting next to me. It was the first time that I had actually seen him. He had singled me out and had followed me for weeks. He took the book from my hand and spoke to me.

-What did he say?

-He said that he found me interesting...intriguing may have been the word that he used. From that day forward, my life changed. He brought me to a different synagogue and introduced me to Orthodox Rabbis. They respected me because of him. I harbored no illusions. And, then, I met my future husband, who was also a Rabbi. Does that shock you, Edward?

-No. In a way, it seems almost fated. Maybe, pre-ordained would be a better term to use.

-Yes! That's how I would put it. Good boy. We *are* in sympathy with each other.

She patted me on the leg and smiled.

-But, Marlena, I've got this gut feeling that your husband is a prop in all of this. Tell me more about your lover.

-There is little left to tell. I moved from my parents' home and became his kept woman. He allowed me to leave my clerk's job. Under his tutelage, I began my serious studies of the occult. Even after I married, I retained my lover for a brief time.

-What did he tell you about the "event?" Was he trying to warn you?

The rain outside let up. I heard the individual drops of water hit the ground: it was a sickening effect of nature as if it were dying and breathing its last bit of life.

-He taught me a great deal about Jewish mysticism and, in particular, about the glyph.

-The other side. The darkness. Don't ask me how I know that.

-You're familiar with it. That's all that matters. Good. I told you that you would eventually answer my question. It was through my knowledge of the glyph that I became a rich woman.

-Tell me more about this mysterious lover of yours.

-When I married, he left me almost immediately, as he said he would. But, he instilled within me the knowledge of life and death that a woman possesses.

-Did he tell you about the "event?" Is that even the right word for it?

-Yes. He did.

-And?

-I grew to fear him.

-Why?

-Every moment became an apprehension of fear and anticipation. I became obsessed with finding out more about it. I grew superstitious. I sought frantically for any clues or information.

-Why and what did he tell you, Marlena? Don't hold out on me.

-To torment me, of course. But, he underestimated me. He made the fatal mistake.

-What did he actually tell you? Level with me.

-That there will be a moment when the scales of heaven and hell will meet and the horizon will be extinguished.

And, then, we heard it. The both of us stood up.

-Did you hear that, Marlena?

-Who's in this room with us? Answer me!

Silence. We both felt it, though. It was a humming sound that touched the tops of our heads. We sat back down. My hostess was agitated.

-Susan thought that she saw someone through the window before.

-He's watching me. I must be close to it now! He's getting anxious. To think that I should have fallen in love with a Jew. It's incomprehensible! Their entire bloodsucking race should have been wiped out! How *dare* he leave me!

I waited a few moments for her to calm down.

-Oh, do forgive my outburst, Edward. As I was saying?

-What was his name?

-His name?

-His name, Marlena. Your lover?

-I've no idea. He never told me. He never told me.

-You expect me to believe that?

The rain had stopped; but, I could feel the dampness.

-Edward, he gave me that information on a Sunday evening: an early part of the evening at a time when our portion of the world begins to turn warm, shortly after the spring equinox. I knew that what he said meant the end of everything. He was surprised that I knew.

-Do you know anything about this man?

-Only that he was a patron of the arts and an intellectual.

-Where did he live? Where did he come from? For God's sake, you must know that much.

-This was his house. He sold it to my husband and myself for a large sum of money. Where did he actually come from? I've no idea. He was a private individual and did not share his confidences.

-He didn't share too much of anything, did he? How did he come to learn what he did?

-Through his own powers of the occult, that must be it.

-I think there's a lot more to it than that.

I looked around the dark cellar.

-Can we open more lights in here?

-No. I prefer the semi-darkness.

-I don't.

-I'm certain that he's watching us at this very moment.

-And, that doesn't bother you? It gives me the creeps.

-I've grown accustomed to it as one does to a fatal disease. It's when I can no longer feel his presence: *that* is when the end will come.

-When you visited your synagogues, Marlena, did you learn anything worthwhile?

-I've taken documents and sacred objects that amounted to very little. However, I've invoked the Gnostic Mass and it-has-been wonderful! It is the only time of day when I feel safe. It is through the Mass that enlightenment and occult power has come to me. And, you will be my priest, that is why you are here. I need a man with balls.

I swallowed another morsel of pot-pie. I was almost afraid to ask my next question.

-Will you be my priestess?

-Of course. My son, Gabriel, will be deacon and Susan will be the Virgin; poor, plain thing; but, it's a part that she's suited for.

I had to ask this next question.

-How do we stop doomsday from happening? Can we stop it from happening?

-Tonight, you will read Valerie's journal and, then, you will tell *me*.

The upstairs door opened and Susan came running down.

-Mother! There are men outside the house.

-The police? How inconvenient. Tell them to go away.

-My mother…no, it's not the police. These men are standing on each corner of the block. Gabriel saw them when he came back from one of your "jobs."

-Don't be impertinent, Miss.

Even though the rain had stopped, the cold crept through my feet and up my body. Marlena took her stockings from my lap and put them on as Susan looked at me in disbelief.

-Our house is surrounded by strange men, who may well mean to murder us all, and my mother stops to put on her nylons.

Her mother's reply was not nice.

-Shut up and get my pocketbook!

Susan ran back upstairs and closed the door behind her.

Marlena fumbled with her nylons, but what she said was plain and distinct.

-This is serious: the four points of the compass have been blocked and soon those men will make their move — and that move is to kill us all, just like Dolores was butchered earlier this evening.

Marlena adjusted her nylons and raced up the stairs as I followed close behind. She threw open the door and looked around wildly with her hair flying in all directions. She ran into the living room. Susan came in with her mother's black, overstuffed bag.

-Give it to me!

She snatched the bag from Susan and rummaged through it like a madwoman. She pulled out a hand pistol.

-Good! Now, we have a chance. Susan get Rosamund and Yolanda and tell your brother to get the car ready. And, get our passports and money. Hurry! And, get some clothes for Edward. He's coming with us.

Susan ran up the stairs. I heard her talking to someone in a calm but hurried voice.

Yolanda came down the stairs looking worried.

-What's this that I hear? The house has been surrounded? What have you done, Marlena? Sweet Edward, you'll protect me, no?

-I'll feel better able to do that as soon as I get some pants on.

-Edward, go upstairs to Erich's room and hurry. There's no time to lose. *Hurry!*

Marlena kept screaming that word "hurry" in an annoyingly high-pitched tone that made me want to slap her across the face. I'm sure that she would have struck me back.

I left the two women alone and hurried upstairs. Too bad that Marlena hadn't told me which room Erich was in. I opened the first door that I came to.

-Erich?

-Yes? You have come for some clothes? We are the same size. Here, I've already put some clothes out for you. We'll talk while you dress, Mr. Mendez.

I flung off the robe and kicked off the slippers. Erich appraised me and nodded. There was nothing sexual in that look: it was a cold appraisal as one man would often give another. Erich was neither threatened by me nor repulsed: an instant camaraderie had been struck up between the two of us. He also noticed the gun I had.

-You carry a German pistol? So do I. Good man.

-Thanks.

-Why are we leaving? I understand that there is danger outside? Wouldn't it be wiser to remain indoors? Tell me of this danger, Mr. Mendez.

I slipped into the underwear and snatched the pants off of the bed.

-Word travels fast in this house. Four men have surrounded the place and Marlena is pretty upset by it. I think she plans to leave the country.

-That ugly woman amuses me. As I expected, she wants to come with us to Germany. Marlena was unable to persuade Rosamund to stay, and so she follows us.

-You may be right about that, Erich; but, I don't think that's why she's leaving at this particular moment.

I sat on the bed and put on Erich's socks.

-I will be honest with you. I am a Nazi. I will also tell you this: beware of Marlena and do not let your guard down. I don't like her, but for me that is not at all unusual for I despise most women.

-Do you know anything about any of this? As one man to another, level with me.

-My Valerie was disturbed by dreams. Rosamund told me that Valerie would lay awake nights because she was fearful of her dreams. And, then-

There was a knock on the door.

Erich shouted through the door.

-We'll be right down!

The person in the hallway walked on.

-Valerie heard things and felt things even when awake. I would laugh at this at the time, but not now. And, this I can tell you, my friend: she confided every-thing to Rosamund and her journal.

I now had on my new friend's white-collared shirt and over it went my shoulder holster and gun.

-I can even lend you my loafers. Here. You look good in my clothes. You haven't forgotten your gun. Good.

-No chance. You wouldn't have a cigarette on you, would you? I left mine in my jacket.

Erich reached into his trouser pocket.

-Here. They're German cigarettes and strong. Take one.

-Thanks.

He took out his lighter and lit it for me.

-So, what do you think of Marlena's children, Mr. Mendez? They're a strange lot, no?

-I've only met her daughter. She seems nice enough and pretty level-headed.

-Yes. I can find no fault with her. Let me know what you think of the son when you meet him. He's strange. I don't like him.

I had to laugh out loud.

-Oh? Is what I said so funny, Mr. Mendez?

-In a way, it is. It seems that Gabriel is unanimously hated. You don't like him. Yolanda doesn't like him. And, your friend, Miss Spender, doesn't like the young man. I almost feel sorry for him.

-Don't. And, Rosamund and I are not friends. She hates me and my beliefs even more.

I made one final check on my gun. Good. The safety catch was on.

I finished dressing and we went downstairs. Erich carried his suitcase with him. The others waited for us at the foot of the stairs. Yolanda had my jacket over her arm and handed it to me.

-Sweet Edward, here's your jacket. It's still a little damp. And, I've already checked: your wallet and cigarettes are there. You see? I look after you.

Marlena made a face at that last remark.

-Let's go. Gabriel has the car parked out in front and I have this!

She had a firm grip on her gun. Something told me that this woman was a crack shot.

Everyone carried a suitcase except for Yolanda and me. We smiled at each other and followed the others out into the night. Marlena's car was a limousine. We piled in: Gabriel and Susan up front, Rosamund,

Yolanda, and Erich on the fold-up seats and Marlena and me in the back.

-Gabriel, to the airport and step on it!

That was Marlena.

The young man floored the gas pedal and we reached the corner in no time. A man in a black coat stood there. He was one of the men I'd seen this afternoon. He turned toward us so that I could see his chalk-white face set against the black night. His head looked disembodied.

Marlena shouted an order at her son.

-Gabriel, run him over!

Gabriel swerved the car to the left and ran over the man. We heard and felt the thud and, for a moment, the man's face crossed the glare of the headlights. The body was flung forward and hit the pavement. Our driver ran over it to finish the job.

His mother turned around to gloat, but her moment of triumph was short-lived. She screamed out her next words.

-He's getting up! The other three are joining him!

Everyone, except Gabriel, turned around to look. He made a sharp right and headed for the airport. Marlena spoke to me.

-I have our passports, Edward.

-You have my passport? How the hell did you get it?

-I sent Gabriel to fetch it this morning. Do you mind?

-You don't miss a trick do you, Marlena?

-Never.

-I'm glad I'm on your side.

-Would you like to accompany us to Germany?

-Do I have a choice?

-Well no, dear boy, you haven't.

Marlena had made our arrangements: illegally and all properly done. We boarded the plane for Munich that night. Surprisingly, Yolanda went with us and, to her astonishment and Marlena's, all of her traveling arrangements had been made, as well.

CHAPTER TEN
THE CONFESSIONAL

I SAT back in the plane seat. In my lap was Valerie's leather-bound journal which Marlena had given to me. I sat next to a sleeping Yolanda and she looked beautiful. I knew that she felt protected by me and drew comfort from my presence. Her hand was on my lap and, gently, I picked it up and slipped past her and into the aisle. I needed to relieve myself. I walked down the narrow aisle and into the rest room. God! that felt good! Now, I could read Valerie's journal in comfort. I opened the door and Marlena was standing there. Why wasn't I surprised?

-I followed you, Edward. We need to finish our conversation. I'll get straight to the point. Sit here: these seats aren't taken.

We sat down.

-Edward…holy places…indeed…why are they holy? Has anyone ever wondered? Really wondered?

She answered her own question.

-They are sanctuaries and links to what we call the unknown. At one time, they were vehicles of transportation to other galaxies: a lost art.

-Go on, Marlena. You've got me hooked.

-I found what I had been after. After so many years, I found it in such a sanctuary!

-Marlena? Your voice…

She leaned closer to me.

-I was in a Catholic church not more than six months ago. Let me tell you what happened.

Marlena told her story, as a story should be told.

-It was an October evening and warm for that time of year. As soon as I climbed the stairs, I knew that something was about to happen. I knew that I was being brought closer to dreaded knowledge. The air was stagnant and had the smell of decay to it. The haze across the sky descended upon the ground like a dark, tattered veil…the ripped shreds from the veil of the temple. I opened the heavy, wooden door and entered the vestibule. It was dark. I saw a man reading something that had been placed on to a bulletin board, and a woman was there with her child. Why do I mention them? Because, I felt that they knew why I had come. I entered the church and saw a few old people lighting candles and saying prayers. It disgusted me to look at them. I detest piety.

-Then, what happened? Don't hold back on me.

-Patience, Edward. Let me tell my story.

Marlena paused for effect.

-I walked down the side aisle and everything looked as if it had been taken from a Master's painting. It was as if the church were shrinking and I was remaining tall. And, then, it felt as if some force were turning me around and pointing me to that particular confessional. I tried turning away; but, I couldn't. Something or someone wanted me to go in there.

She stopped and looked down at her hands.

-I entered and closed the confessional door behind me and knelt down. This is what happened.

-Bless me, Father, for I have sinned. Counsel me and forgive your daughter.

-In the name of the Father and of the Son and of the Holy Ghost. Amen. Tell me of your sins.

-They are far too numerous to mention.

-Speak to me.

-I hesitate to speak of them. They may shock you.

-I am waiting. Tell me of your greatest sin.

-I seek-

-I know what it is that you seek.

-Indeed.

-You fear death. You fear the destruction.

-How do you know that? Tell me, priest.

-I know who you are and why you were brought here.

-Who the hell are you?

-Before this night is done, I will be dead.

-Talk to me outside.

-No. Don't look upon my face or you would run from this place. Her name is Valerie Spender: seek her out in Germany, but hurry, dearest Marlena. It may already be too late.

-How do you know me? Who are you?

-Go to this young girl before she is killed. She will be murdered, and for this they shall burn in hell! I will see to it!

-Tell me who you are. I demand to know.

-A fiend in the nightmares that you cannot allow yourself to remember even a glimmer of. I am a doomed soul who has lost his lust for immortality and now seeks to redeem myself within the great Judgment Hall. For my grievous misdeeds, I will be trampled upon, but one god will take pity and judge me. I am a distortion of what life may one day be. I am the wretch who walks upon the bodies of the dead so that no one may hear my footsteps. Beware, Marlena, for I am evil.

-I went to his booth, Edward, and yanked the door open. He was kneeling down and wearing a black coat. He turned his face to me and it was hideous. *Hideous!* Burnt white and old beyond belief...lips which oozed blood. He got up and knocked me to the floor. I heard him run down the aisle.

I took a deep breath before I spoke.

-Marlena, was he one of those murdering goons we've been running into?

-He was much more than that. And he was right about everything.

-He was probably killed for what he did.

-Probably.

-But, why did he do it? Why? What was he getting out of it? What was in it for him? Salvation?

-Maddening, isn't it? I've wondered several thousand times, myself. A last act of redemption? Revenge?

-It sounds like his conscience was bothering him.

-The only way to know is to find out who these men are.

-I wouldn't call them "men." I don't know what I'd call them.

-Anyway, dear boy, go back to your seat and read Valerie's journal. I'll get you some java.

I went back to my seat and climbed over Yolanda. I reached down and drew out the journal from the duffel bag that I'd bought at the airport. Instead of reading it, I rested it on my lap. I had to close my eyes to think and make some sense out of what had gone on in the last two days. I had no past and, according to Marlena, the future wouldn't last much beyond the end of the month.

No past and no future, but what did these words matter? They were only a frame to place experience on, nothing more and nothing less. The future was one of rolled-up parchments, some would disintegrate to the touch while others would be held up to the light of day so that the purity of the sun's rays could extinguish any evil.

-Psst! Edward, dear boy, your java. It's strong. I've put some sugar in it.

Marlena passed me the large, white cup and went back to her own seat. I drank the coffee. Marlena had put some cinnamon in it, as well

The present...yes...what had to be done in the here and now outweighed all the forgotten yesterdays: it outstripped whatever priorities of life I had once had. Something would occur near the end of April that would somehow erase everything that had gone before.

I opened Valerie's journal and began to read...and stopped. I sat back and drank some more of the coffee. I heard the airplane's propellers and felt the confinement of the plane. In one sense, it was a comfort to be carried along and far away from a dangerous place, but to where? To a place closer to the truth? Were we in safety or were we trapped within a hull of metal that propelled us toward nowhere?

I glanced over to my left. Yolanda was still asleep or pretending to be. Marlena leaned forward in her seat and stared at me. I drank some more coffee and opened the journal, again. Why did I keep hesitating? My right finger still felt that pressure. It never left me. And, the scent on my body that even my shower hadn't gotten rid of. It wasn't cologne. It wasn't a man's fragrance of any kind. It was something to intoxicate the senses in bed. Yolanda had loved it.

-Edward?

-I thought you were asleep, baby.

-Only pretending. What did Marlena want?

-Advice on reading Valerie's journal.

-You keep putting it down. Why? Are you afraid of what you'll find out? I am.

-Maybe, I am too. You know me pretty good, don't you?

-I think you should read it. But, I'm afraid of what you'll find out. If it's too frightening, don't tell me.

-I may have to, baby. But, why don't you go back to sleep? You need your rest. It's been a pretty eventful day.

-For you, too. I'll sleep on your shoulder. Do you mind?

-No.

-Open the journal. Just get it over with. I'll close my eyes and try to sleep.

I kissed Yolanda on the forehead. She snuggled up closer and I took comfort from that. Too bad I couldn't smoke. I put a cigarette in my mouth, anyway.

I looked down at Valerie's journal. I opened it and began to read the dead girl's words.

CHAPTER ELEVEN
VALERIE

THE WAR was over and another winter was about to begin. It's wonderful to feel the cold, fresh air and to see people come back to life even if many buildings still remain destroyed.

Erich is coming by this morning to fetch me along to my recital. I'll wear my winter-white dress and shoes to match. I want to get up; but, I know that Rosamund is bringing my breakfast up to me. I insisted that I felt perfectly fine and would enjoy eating in our kitchen. I am not a good liar.

My dreams disturbed me, again. I woke up last night and listened to the voices, but their sound was masked by terrible music. I could feel it penetrate my body as though an electrical current had seized me. It might have been organ music, but it was debased and unholy, blaspheming anything that it touched. I had gotten up to look out the window and saw where it was coming from: the dark side of the moon. The dark light that hangs in the night sky. It's a beacon that was placed there by the fallen angel as a guiding specter for souls on their departure from this earth and as a temptation for those souls still remaining within the temple of their body.

Evil thing.

If it were only gone from the sky, the stars would shine more brightly and the waters of the world would know a calm and reflect the beauty of the heavens.

Last night, I also had a vision.

I was in a room in a deserted city. The sun had just set.

-Valerie, let me turn on the lamp, dear. You'll hurt your eyes reading in the dark like that.

I was seated on a chair that was overstuffed with down feathers and, in my hands, was a copy of Cervantes' work.

-Thank you, Max, that's very sweet of you.

-Nothing at all, really. Do you mind if I join you? You shouldn't be by yourself.

-Of course not.

Max sat down on the couch and pulled his brown, tweed jacket closer about him.

-Are you warm enough like that, Valerie?

-No, Max. I think I'll get my sweater.

A woman walked in with piles of blonde hair on her head that were somehow pinned into place. She spoke to me.

-No need to, dear. I have your sweater right here. I thought you might need it.

-Thank you, Irene.

Another woman walked in: an older woman.

-And, I brought in some hot cocoa for you. I made it myself.

-Thank you, Rose, that was very thoughtful of you.

I looked out the window and saw how dark it had become. The evening had turned into night so quickly.

-It's a clear night outside even though I can't see anything but the moon.

That was Melody. I knew her, even though I had never met her before. She sat on the window ledge and looked outside into the darkness. Melody held the lace curtain in her hand.

-What do you see, Melody? How can it be a clear night when there is nothing to be seen in the universe any longer? Can emptiness contain a clarity in it? Perhaps, it can.

It was Oshido who had spoken. He sat cross-legged in his chair, wearing a black kimono of silk.

Melody spoke as if to herself.

-I see the moon and clusters of stars about it. It's like a halo of white, milky crystal. It's almost too beautiful to be our moon.

Max spoke.

-Maybe, it isn't. But, I'd get away from that window, luv. It might shatter.

A vibration filled the house and for me it was deafening. It was a sound that no mortal should hear.

Irene smiled at me.

-We're used to it, dear. Don't let it worry you.

-Can I interest anyone in a drink?

-Bring me a double vodka, Sean, please. I am so nervous. I don't know where I am. I am trembling! Look at my hands and how they shake. Please hurry with my drink.

-But, you do know where you are, Yvonne. I do.

-I do not know, I tell you! You see how Sean crucifies me, Michael? Take pity on poor Yvonne. I beg you!

Michael drank his beer, not listening to Yvonne's tirade.

In the far corner stood Abraham, like a shadow standing in the dark. He pointed to something in the opposite corner that looked like a grotesque imitation of a mannequin's head.

The light in the room went out, but someone spoke. It was the mannequin's head that was speaking. It was absurd and frightening to watch its mouth move.

-He did it. He killed me.

Melody moved away from the window and walked toward what was left of Becky.

I could now see everyone, but there was no longer any room. There was just a backdrop of blackness that spread itself all about us.

-Who did this to you, Becky?

-Yeah, Becky, answer Melody. Just point a finger.

That was one of the men laughing. It might have been Sean. I think it was.

-He'll have you murdered, Valerie, too. He won't do it himself. He'll have his henchmen do it for him.

Becky uttered those last words, closed her eyes, and died. A foot kicked her head so hard that the entire motion was a blur.

The darkness…the cold…the air turned to ice.

I stood still, but lost my balance. My hand touched down on to ice. It was smooth, white ice that stretched into infinity.

I heard the sound of scraping on the ice as a distant figure came toward me. It was a young girl in a light blue costume. As she skated closer, I could see that she was a Spanish beauty. She didn't stop, but circled about me.

-The art of dying is an art that's quite serene. So many before us have made this transition: a countless number and, yet, the number is countable. But, don't be afraid, Valerie, for it's a sharp pain and, then, release.

She skated away. I could see the pretty diamond clasp that kept her hair in place. She looked over her shoulder at me.

-I'll send Edward, but not to you. I'll send him to me as a last hope, for one must play the game, no? You don't say much, do you? I don't blame you.

She skated away.

I was alone.

I heard Rosamund coming. She knocked on the door and walked in.

-And, how is my sister on this beautiful morning?

-I am fine, Rosamund. Let me help you with the tray.

-No. I am perfectly capable of carrying a breakfast tray on my own, thank you. Now, please sit up and let me spoil my little sister.

Rosamund was always so kind to me.

My mind wandered back to my vision of last night. It had been a vision of a dead world and of an unrecorded moment in history. A moment that had not yet occurred? Am I to help prevent something from occurring?

-Did you sleep well last night, Valerie?

-No.

-I am glad that you don't try to conceal it from me.

I jumped out of bed and began to dress.

-You are going to wear your white dress, again. You waited for the war to be over and that was the right thing to do. Here. Put on your pretty gold medallion. The one that I bought for you from that man in Rome.

-Yes. It was just before the war. Do you remember what he said about it?

-Yes. It frightened me for some reason. It was in the open marketplace near the Coliseum.

-He said that it was from ancient Sumer: a civilization that pre-dated Egypt.

-That man was odd. He was not what he appeared to be.

-I don't know what you mean, Rosamund. He-

-It was he who sought us out in the marketplace. Yes. It is clear to me now. But, why? What did he want from us?

The doorbell rang.

-I am expecting no one.

The sunlight seemed wrong. It was too white. It was like the color of a child's garment who has just died.

The doorbell rang, again, and this time the sunlight did fade.

It was the first omen that the end of the world was near.

-I must see who it is, Valerie. Wait here. Don't leave the room.

Rosamund ran down the stairs to answer the door. Only a few moments passed when she came running back up the stairs.

-Someone is playing a joke on us and it is not funny! I do not appreciate such humor.

Rosamund was frightened.

They were watching us.

Rosamund paced the floor. I was afraid to say anything. I noticed something in her hand. It was a piece of paper which she slipped into her pocket.

-Come, Valerie, we must leave soon or we'll be late. We can't wait for Erich. I'll call for a cab.

When we arrived at the theatre, Erich was at the back entrance waiting for us. He took me into his arms and kissed me.

-Valerie, we must hurry inside.

Rosamund separated us and led the way to the waiting room. Erich followed us in. He wasn't the type to be put off.

-Get out, Erich. You have no business being here. You will make Valerie nervous and she needs to be calm before a performance.

-I will do as I like. You don't give orders to me.

-How unfortunate for the both of us. Now, get out or I will call the police and have you thrown out.

Erich slumped down on to the couch next to me.

-You have not asked me why I did not come to your house this morning, Rosamund.

-It never occurred to me.

-I saw what happened.

-What are you saying to me? And, for all of our sakes, I pray that you are speaking the truth, Erich.

-I only speak the truth.

-Liar.

-I saw the man who dropped off that note as I was coming down the street. I ran after the swine because he looked suspicious to me. There was something about him which I did not trust and which made me uneasy.

-And? Or do you want to keep us in suspense for your own pleasure?

-Rosamund?

-Yes, Valerie? What is it?

-It's almost time for me to go on stage.

-Of course.

Rosamund fussed with my dress as Erich looked on in amusement. My sister opened the door. I walked out into the wing of the theater to be called. It was so strange. I could still hear Rosamund and Erich talking. It was foreboding. It was another sign that things were not as they should be. My world was losing its sanity and I was powerless to stop the destruction.

-Well, Erich, finish what you were about to say.

-Will you tell Valerie, or will I have to? I will, you know.

-Finish your story, please. I would like to see my sister-

-I could not catch him. He ran so fast. I did not expect that. I expected a clumsy oaf whom I could easily overpower.

-That would have pleased you, no doubt.

-The man was wearing a black trench-coat. He was not tall. I am taller. I caught a glimpse of his ugly face. How could such an old and clumsy man escape me?

-That, Erich, is a very good question.

I walked out on to the stage. I was so nervous that I practically hid myself behind the piano. I curtsied to the Master of Ceremonies and, then, to the audience. I sat down at the piano.

Rosamund sat next to Erich on the couch and fidgeted with her bracelet.

-Show me the note, Rosamund. Then, perhaps we can make something of all this.

-Here.

-Interesting. I will read it aloud.

"Your sister will soon be murdered. I cannot stop this event. It is one in a series of events in which I am helpless. A woman will come looking for Valerie, but she will be too late. Her name is Marlena Lake."

I played Chopin's Polonaise Brilliant. It was not what I had intended to play. The notes filled the air of the concert hall.

-Do you know this Marlena Lake, Erich? Valerie has never mentioned her to me.

-Perhaps, Valerie's only chance is herself. She must open up to us. She is a threat to persons unknown: dangerous persons. I have an instinct about such things.

I had completed the opening melody when I saw them: each one stood in a corner of the theater...the four men...the four corners of destruction and creation. That's how it would happen: by means of the compass when the sun will set and the crescent moon will rise in the heavens.

But, what was I saying? That wasn't me speaking. Why should I know this? The words were beautiful, but their meaning was horrible.

Those men kept staring at me. They nodded to each other and plotted.

Rosamund!

Erich!

Help me!

These men are going to kill me!

I looked at the audience in panic, but all they saw was my smiling face.

Help me! Anyone!

-Let us go out and watch Valerie.

-Yes. But, let us hurry, Erich! Something is not right. I feel that my sister is calling out to me.

Rosamund!

They're moving now. They set their bloodless eyes on me and not on each other anymore. The man at the far corner moved down the aisle. The man opposite him moved closer to the stage. The other two, closest to the stage, climbed up the steps. I saw their ruined and ancient faces.

One of them looked up and the lights started to dim. There was a murmur in the audience.

Why can't I move?

Rosamund and Erich were now standing in the wings.

-Valerie is almost finished- what is that man doing over there? The lights! They are so dim! I must go out there to her.

-You'll make an idiot of yourself, Rosamund.

-Get away from me.

Rosamund ran out on to the stage.

-Get away from her! Stop! Stop, you! Get-away-from-my-sister!

Rosamund rushed toward the approaching man and struck him in the face. It was a hard blow and the fiend staggered back against the piano and the lid crashed down. The audience stood up almost in unison as people began to scream.

-Valerie! Run to Erich!

I stood up and screamed as the other fiend came at me. This time, the audience panicked and struggled to get into the aisles. A gunshot was heard and the fiend who was coming at me staggered and fell into the audience. It was Erich who had fired the shot. He never missed a target. He didn't miss this time. Erich ran on to the stage and fired another shot as the fiend stood up.

The audience was a mass of hysteria and fear with people crushing each other in their struggle to get out toward the imagined safety of the street. People were being trampled and shoved about.

Rosamund, who had held on to the other fiend, was thrown to the floor. This one jumped off the stage and joined his three companions. They cleared a path for themselves through the crowd, knocking people to the ground and against the wall and back on to the chairs. But, a few brave souls in the audience fought back. A woman managed to stab one of the fiends with her hat pin right between the eyes. It screamed in agony but kept pushing its way through. A young man belted one in the face and blood spurted in all directions.

The four monsters escaped.

The lights went back up, but the panic had not subsided. Erich, Rosamund, and I fled from the theater. We rushed to a cafe that was a few blocks away.

-Useless to call in the police. What could they do? Nothing. And, besides, I don't trust them. They only do things for their own gain: a better and more efficient police force is needed.

-You are right, Erich; but, something must be done. An attempt has been made on Valerie's life and to do nothing-

-We must examine all of our options. And, as I perceive the matter, we have only two.

-What are they?

-Valerie, you must tell us everything. And that woman, Marlena Lake…we must contact her.

Rosamund looked doubtful about that last option. She wasn't trusting of strangers and to trust a woman whom she had never met was not a thing to be entered into lightly.

-Valerie, you must tell us everything that you know.

-And, you must not leave anything out!

-Lower your voice, Erich.

-What do I care if people are listening? I fear none of them.

-We must be careful. Tell us, Valerie, what does all this mean?

-I don't know what any of it means, not really. But, I do know where it will all end. The end of the world is coming. It will end on a clear and beautiful spring day.

Rosamund and Erich struggled to catch their breath.

-What are you telling us? How will this happen? What will cause such an event? You must tell us, Valerie. In the name of all that is holy, we must try and stop it!

-He will do it…the man in the bar…the deceiver.

-Tell us why he will do this…this deceiver.

-To turn the coin around.

Erich had recovered his breath.

-You speak in riddles. Speak plainly, I order you!

-The glyph will be inverted.

-Rosamund, look at her. She speaks as if in a trance.

-I am not in a trance, Erich. It will be awful and quick. My dreams have told me all this; not in words, but in tones. I hear strange music when I sleep and even when I'm awake. It's like a pressure of electricity over my body. It all comes from the moon. The moon will be the graveyard of our world.

We stayed in the cafe for a long time. We were not even safe in crowded areas. Why had they chosen to try and kill me in broad daylight and in front of so many people? I knew how Erich would answer that question: as a demonstration of power.

-What is the name of this deceiver?

-He is an outcast among his own people. He walked the world once, but by another man's side who was a good man.

-Oh? And, was he a Jew?

-He was one with the world and with God.

-How very nice for him. But, why was he traveling with a destroyer of people, eh?

-Don't bully her, Erich.

-I am not bullying her. I simply want answers.

-He knew of him and was never tempted by him.

Erich spit on the floor.

-That's *his* story.

It was late afternoon when we boarded the cab for home. Erich came with us and stayed for dinner. After dinner, Erich and I were left alone in the dining room for a few minutes.

-I feel that I should stay the night with you. Of course, I will sleep down here on the sofa; but, all you need do is to call out and I will be with you instantly.

-But, Erich, that could be-

-Dangerous? I don't care. I can take care of myself and, besides, I have my gun with me. Not even Rosamund can object to my staying

Erich slept on the sofa in the living room downstairs. Rosamund insisted that I sleep in her room.

-So, how do you feel? Tired? I don't blame you.

-Rosamund? Maybe, we should have gone to the police. Maybe, they could have helped us.

-They couldn't help us. How? And, what would we tell them? Nothing. Those four men approached the stage and two of them walked up on to it: so what? They carried no weapons with them, did they? It is Erich who would have had the explaining to do by shooting a man.

-But, they attacked you.

-I struck the first blow. Let's not talk of it anymore. Tomorrow, if you still want to, we will go to the police. I promise.

Rosamund turned the light off The street lamp outside cast its light on the bedroom floor.

I looked at my sister lying next to me in bed. Anyone near me was in danger. I knew that as soon as Rosamund was asleep, I would have to leave her room and go into my own bedroom.

I got up and looked out the window. I saw the crescent moon in the night sky. Diana's bow lit that tiny portion of the sky, and the stars behind it were the ornaments that her fellow gods wore on their garments of black velvet. I felt safe with Diana in the sky. I knew that she would look after me and protect me in the life to come after death. She would place my medallion of pure gold about my neck and dangling from that ornament would be a golden arrow whose brilliance would drive away the evil that was always drawn to the light.

I left my sister's room. For a moment, I stood in the hallway and listened. Then, I rushed to my room and flung open the door. I didn't put on the light. The window was open and the curtain was pulled to one side. I walked over to the window to see Diana's bow, again. Her arrow would pierce the hearts of my transgressors, but this would be done to avenge my murder.

I laid down on my bed and waited. Was this wrong of me? Yes! I sat up. I wouldn't just be murdered!

I ran to the window and screamed to Diana for help.

-Diana, help me to live. Help me to do what is right in this life.

Rosamund heard my cries into the heavens. I heard her run down the corridor and call out my name.

-Valerie! Open the door and let me in!

I hadn't locked the door.

I glanced at the moon. All around it were clouds gathering, but Diana's bow was untouched.

I went to the door, but a shadow stood in front of it.

Erich banged his fists against the door and cursed at the top of his lungs.

I saw another shadow in the corner. It moved. I saw this shadow only because it was blacker than the surrounding darkness. It moved toward me. I backed away from it. Another shadow was in another corner of the room. It moved closer to me. I moved toward the window. I turned to jump out, but another shadow was there with its arms outstretched.

I was trapped.

I screamed.

-Rosamund! Erich! Look for Diana's bow and arrow. When the moon and the sun can be seen at opposite horizons- trust Marlena and Edward. My medallion-

A cold, wet hand grabbed me. I struggled, but its touch nauseated me. The other two fiends came to help it do its deed. The one at the door stayed there with its arms outstretched like a black cross blocking the way of Rosamund and Erich.

I was dragged to the bed and pinned down. The other fiend was standing in mid-air near to the ceiling which looked higher than it should be. In his hands was a long, metal rod aimed at my chest. I saw his blackened eyes stare down at me. He flung the rod at me and, at that moment, I was taken from my body. I was lifted up and I could feel Diana's presence. The fiends fled from her. They left my lifeless body behind.

From my soul's body, I saw Rosamund and Erich burst into the room. Rosamund screamed. Erich ran about the room looking for someone to kill. His gun was drawn. Out of sheer frustration, he fired a bullet into the ceiling. He fired another bullet and, then, another one. Rosamund knelt down next to the bed and touched my neck. Erich shouted at the top of his lungs.

-She's dead. Why do you waste your time?

Rosamund got up and looked at Erich.

-Yes. My sister is dead. But, take solace, Erich, and go to one of your other women.

-I need nothing from you or from any woman.

-And, now, we must call for the police, Erich.

-And, then?

-We wait for Marlena Lake. Only she can save the world.

PART THREE: ARMAGEDDON

CHAPTER TWELVE
STRATEGY

THE HANDWRITING in Valerie's journal had changed. Someone else's hand had written those last few pages. Was it Rosamund? No. Not her style. Marlena? Yes. I almost laughed with the certainty that I felt about this. Marlena would piece together the fragments of Valerie's last day and write it down as if she, herself, were actually living it. And, she was probably pretty close to the mark.

I leaned over in my seat. Marlena was still watching me. Christ! Did this woman never rest? She got up and went to the back of the plane. She beckoned me to follow her. I tried to get up without awakening Yolanda. I slid out of the seat and noticed that Susan was not in her seat. I walked to the back of the plane and tried to balance myself in the narrow and dark aisle. Marlena and Susan waited for me. I looked out the window and saw that we were crossing over an area of land.

-Edward, sit down. We're almost at the airport and we haven't much time. What did you think of Valerie's journal? And, don't say that it was interesting. Tell me something that I don't know.

-That part about the crescent moon and Diana's bow. I found that strange and-

-Go on!

-It's a clue, Marlena. I think Valerie gave us the time of month, if not the exact day, when to expect the end of the world.

-Dear boy, tell me more.

-I can't be sure, but I think it'll happen in the early evening that comes just before dusk. It will be on the moon's waxing cycle to a full moon. I think.

-No. You feel it as do I.

Susan spoke in her usual calm and logical voice.

-I've already looked up this date in the charts: it's on April 29th, just over three weeks away, on Friday at dusk. The sun and the crescent moon will be in direct opposition to each other.

-Okay. We know *when* it'll happen, but exactly what the hell is going to happen? How will the world come to an end? Fire? A biblical flood? An Atomic war?

-You tell me, Edward. Speak through your soul and tell us. And, remember, Valerie knew you. She knew that you would come to us.

I sat back and said the first thing that came into my head.

-The plague of Seth will overtake the world.

Marlena gasped and gripped her pocketbook.

-Go on! *Go on!*

-The centers of hearts and the hordes of locusts.

Susan touched my arm.

-Are you all right, Edward? You look as if you've just seen a ghost.

-I feel drained of energy…wiped out. How do we stop it? *How?* I had a vision of giant insects ravaging the landscape. My God! It was horrible. What in God's name can we do to stop it?

Marlena sat back in her seat with a look of determination.

-Through magic, Edward. Through magic and power we'll stop it.

-You mean through cunning, mother, don't you?

-Yes.

We had been in Germany one week when I realized that I was now a dependent of Marlena's. I was one of her group. My ego should have resisted.

The seven of us were seated in Rosamund's living room. I didn't like her house. It was small and cluttered with papers all over the place, most of it sheet music. The place needed a good paint job and some modern furniture.

It was late afternoon. No one in the room looked even remotely at ease. Marlena had called us there and now we waited for her to begin. She was exactly where she so loved to be: the center of attention. She appraised everyone in the room: Yolanda, myself, and Susan who were seated on the couch, Erich who was on the floor, and Rosamund and Gabriel on the piano bench.

Marlena was in the easy chair with her black patent leather pocketbook in her lap Her glances kept darting to the window.

-Well, to begin with, we have about two weeks left. We must act at the precise moment if we are to be successful. And, of course, I will be.

-Oh? And, when is that, mother?

-Don't be flippant with me, young lady, or I'll smack you right in the face. As I was saying...

Yolanda addressed Marlena in a coy and bantering voice.

-Yes? What were you saying, Marlena? I don't seem to remember.

-Why don't you leave? You have no business here. And, quite frankly, I can't stand the sight of you.

- It's not too pleasant from here, either. I know of a fabulous coterie. I'm sure that she would be able to do something.

Rosamund interrupted this bickering.

-We are wasting time sitting around and arguing while the world rushes toward its doom.

Marlena looked hard at Yolanda.

-I intend to save us all. And, there is a traitor here: a rotten, little spy! I won't have it!

Yolanda took a personal offense at this.

-How dare you? I'm no one's spy. I'm here with my boyfriend. Is that so difficult for you to understand? Perhaps, it is.

Rosamund spoke before Marlena could launch a verbal attack on Yolanda.

-What must we do, Miss Lake?

-I know what Mass must be performed, but it's the location which eludes me.

Susan spoke to her mother, but kept glancing over at Yolanda.

-I think it should be in Egypt or, perhaps, Athens. But, I lean more toward Egypt or possibly Iran, the cradle of the Garden: it's said to be a gravitational power center, and there is the energy of antiquity stored there. The sands of the desert physically contain fragments of vibration...of history, actually. In time, science will bear that out.

-Good girl! Mother is proud of you.

It was my turn to join in.

-Marlena, what are we doing for the next two weeks? Hiding out won't do any good. They're probably keeping tabs on us right now.

-To answer your question: keeping ourselves alive which is not so easy, Edward. And, the preparations for the coming ritual will take that long. There are many details to attend to. You will have to be trained, dear boy. Susan will help you and, of course, I'll supervise your entire training.

I shook my head.

-What's wrong, Edward?

-Marlena, I still have a lot of doubts about this. I'm not so sure of what it is we're dealing with and what will happen if we fail.

-All will be taken and the course of this planet's destiny will be altered. It's vibration will waver and change and eventually be brought back, but never toward the orbit of God.

That was Rosamund who had just spoken.

Erich stared at her.

-That sounded more like your sister, Valerie, than you.

Rosamund clutched her throat, struggling with her emotions.

-I felt my sister's heartbeat. She is with us...helping us! Listen! I hear her playing the piano. It's what she played on her last day on earth! Can't you hear it?

Marlena was not impressed.

-Get a grip on yourself. My plans are set. In Cairo, we'll meet in two weeks and the deadliest Mass of all time will be performed.

Yolanda smiled coyly.

-Marlena, may I attend?

-Of course, my dear. I wouldn't dream of having it without you.

-Rosamund?

-Yes, Mr. Mendez?

-Would you mind if I had a look around your sister's room?

-Why?

My answer to this bitch surprised even me.

-I think you're holding out on us, lady, that's why.

-I don't know what you mean.

-I think you do. Was your sister-

-Yes?

-An artist?

-I think it is you who are holding out on me, Mr. Mendez. Yes. Valerie loved to sketch and was quite good at it.

-Do you mind if I go on up? I won't disturb anything.

-Do as you like. It doesn't matter. Valerie's room is the first door to your right at the top of the stairs.

I got up and made to leave the room.

-I'll be right back. Yolanda? Stay put, baby.

I headed up the narrow flight of carpeted stairs. I opened the door and walked in. The bedroom was small and neat and feminine. The scent in the air was subtle but unmistakably that of a sea breeze. I went over to the bureau which had a mirror. I caught a glimpse of myself. I placed my hands on the bureau and stared at my reflection. What the- On the bureau was a small pile of papers. I picked them up. Sketches...about a dozen of them. I recognized Rosamund. Valerie had drawn several of her sister. Erich's sketch was also there. And so was mine and Yolanda's.

No doubt about it: the girl had been a genuine clairvoyant for all the good it had done her.

The last sketch was that of a bartender...no...a young man tending bar and serving a beautiful woman. Who were they? Were they the people in Valerie's journal? That must be it. But, what was the connection? This particular sketch was dark. It was like midnight closing in on the two people. And, the young man's eyes were almost alive and staring at me. It wasn't a friendly stare either. No. There was downright evil in his eyes.

The nest few weeks were the most extraordinary weeks of my life or, more accurately put, the brief part of this life that I could recall. Marlena and Susan taught me the arts of the sacred and ancient Mass: a ritual that was in part founded on the Egyptian rites of the dead and on an even more ancient civilization: Sumer.

Susan's and Marlena's care of me was meticulous: neither woman ever left my side. With Susan, I didn't mind this so much because she was a careful and thorough teacher. She insisted that it was all science: a science that did not require any apparatus save the electrical currents of thought focused through the human brain.

Marlena, on the other hand, was a ruthless teacher who taught by constant repetition, and there was a huge amount to repeat. And, she was always prodding me about my past. She never let up on this. She wanted to know my purpose in life and to what end did I seek knowledge. I couldn't answer any of this; but, they were questions which forced me to think about myself and how I had gotten on to that slab of ice. Had I been manipulated from the beginning?

We were in Egypt with only three days to go until the Mass. Marlena, Susan, Gabriel, Yolanda, and myself were at an outdoor cafe having lunch. The weather was hot and dry and we were sitting in a shaded area. I wore a white kaftan and sandals. Marlena remarked on my fitting in so well with our surroundings: the mark of a true occultist.

-A sorcerer's task is not to call attention to himself. He must be a chameleon of sorts and able to fit in with his surroundings in order that he may control them and those within his sphere.

-What do you mean by "control," Marlena?

-Altering whatever one wishes to alter or annihilate, Edward.

-Mother, have you annihilated anyone, lately?

-Ask me that question in a few days, my dear.

-Assuming that we have a few days left, Marlena.

-Dear Yolanda, I will be victorious. I won't have it any other way.

-Pretty sure of yourself, no?

-Yes, Yolanda, I am.

Marlena almost choked on her gin.

Yolanda and Susan laughed.

-Water, mother? Choking to death?

-Now, what was I saying? I was commenting on how Edward fits in with his surroundings. I can feel the energy coming from him even now. It feels glorious! We will win!

A few patrons turned to stare at us.

-Marlena?

-Yes, Edward?

-Why did you pack Rosamund off the way you did?

-Do you miss her?

-No. I didn't find her to be all that friendly.

-She wasn't very interesting. She was a bitch.

-Yolanda, we agree. She was a bore. We're better off without her and her Nazi friend.

-My mother…

Gabriel drank his coffee and, as usual, had nothing to say. Susan looked over her shoulder.

-Are you all right, Susan?

-No, Edward. I'm not. We're being watched.

I could see that Marlena was trying not to look around.

-My daughter is paranoid.

-Isn't that the pot calling the kettle black, mother?

She ignored her daughter because she probably couldn't argue with the truth.

-Rosamund and Erich had to be left behind. Erich had no part in this drama. Rosamund is far too emotional and knew more than she was willing to tell. I should have killed the bitch. How foolish of me not to.

-Why kill a bore, Marlena?

-She was a threat to us, Yolanda. She may, in fact, go to the police. Anyway, Edward, still can't remember anything of your past?

-Oh, mother, give it a rest! Really. We're asking enough of this man as it is.

-That's okay, Susan. Not my past, Marlena; but I keep seeing a group of people at a table in a bar somewhere. When I was reading Valerie's journal, the people who she mentioned in it were familiar to me. Their names triggered some kind of memory.

-What were you doing at the table, Edward. Tell me. You *must* remember.

-I don't know. We weren't drinking or even talking.

-You were conducting a seance. *That's* how you were sent back to this time and place.

-But, Marlena, if I was sent back to the past, doesn't that mean that there's a future?

-A future that has somehow been distorted and changed. A plague had somehow overtaken the world.

-How?

-I've a vague idea, Edward; but after the Mass, we might have a few answers.

-Where will the Mass take place?

-Thinking of joining us, Yolanda?

-You said that I could. You promised.

-Of course, dear, a witness is needed. You merely sit there and look pretty.

-Marlena, where?

-Within the area of the great pyramid and right before dusk, Edward.

-Do you think there'll be any attempt to stop us?

-I don't think so. The attempt will be made during the Mass. He'll try to kill me; but, it won't matter because if I fail, the world comes to an end anyway. And, do you know what will be the most horrible part? No one will be aware of it. It will happen so quickly and ruthlessly that in an instant it will be over and a new world will take its place that will be a carbon copy of this one. But, the circumstances will be different as the very glue which holds this planet of ours together will come unglued, so to speak, for a moment. A new race will be substituted for the old one: a race born from the- I can't even bring myself to say it.

We waited for our "leader" to continue.

-At times, you know, I've thought of just allowing it all to happen or, perhaps, taking refuge somewhere and just witnessing the event. But, there is no refuge. How could there be? For a single moment, the wave of time will be disrupted and a new order will take hold. It will be the expelling of one consciousness for another. And, you may ask what will become of the consciousness that was once ours? Consciousness is energy that cannot just be driven out or annihilated. No. It must go somewhere.

-Dare I ask where, Marlena?

-Into the chasm, Yolanda, that we call the abyss: the dark nothingness that leads…somewhere.

-Oh, where?

-Dear Yolanda. Here, of course. The very seat that you're sitting on now. Consciousness doesn't die. He can't destroy it. It forced Edward back here to me. And, somehow, my dear, you are involved.

Yolanda and I found the implications of Marlena's statements disturbing.

-I'm suddenly quite thirsty. Gabriel, fetch mother another gin, would you, please? That's a good boy. And, only a smidgen of tonic water.

Gabriel sprang to his feet to get the gin, but despite outward appearances, that young man wasn't a mama's boy.

-Marlena, why me and Yolanda? How are we connected? Did we know each other in a past life?

-No, Edward, you knew each other in a future life. Somehow, Yolanda brought you here. It was no accident your appearance in the ice rink. It was planned.

-Who planned it?

-Interestingly enough, I believe it was Yolanda.

CHAPTER THIRTEEN
THE TIME DECEIVER

I HAD been going to bed early these past few days because my body and mind were drained by day's end. Now, I just laid on top of the sheets, naked and with thoughts of Yolanda. Nice. I turned my head toward the right to look at the magnificent view of the desert. I stared into the vastness of the ancient gods' realm. It was a landscape that had been changed by the elements of nature and the meanderings of man. The sun touched the horizon. This burning sphere would soon sink below the desert's rim, pushed by the sacred chariot only to re-emerge the next day and begin its journey once again, renewed and traversing the golden arc across the blue desert sky.

The cold, desert air wafted over my body. It caressed that manhood that was mine and it brought me to excitement. I felt the cool and caressing touch of a woman's hand...the hand of a temple priestess. Her body reached through time and space to kneel down beside me. Her lips felt like two small drops of frost as they caressed my hard, throbbing rod. Her tongue was selfish as was her disciplined passion...so disciplined and so strong. I felt hurt and pain, but this was a joy as I cried out and as she drank the life giving sperm that I thought would choke her.

And, she was gone.

I turned my back toward the desert as I got up and out of bed to walk toward the window. I was still sensitive in that sacred area. I took a deep breath of the night air. Only one more day and I would know everything or I would be as nothing that had never existed. The concept, for me, was impossible to grasp; but, somehow, I felt that Marlena had grasped its implications.

Tomorrow was a strange word to use because it denoted time and time is running out and there will literally be no time left. There will be nothing left. The great sea will no longer have ripples upon its surface. Instead, the life-giving waters of the primal sea will be a stagnant pool of lifeless nothing.

As the sun sank beneath the horizon, it stirred some memory within one who hasn't yet lived a life to which he won't return. If we succeed, I'll stay here and, if not...no point in thinking about that.

I wrapped my arms about my torso. I gazed at the beautiful, cold stars of the night that gave no warmth to my body. I must be satisfied with their distance.

Diana's bow was suspended in the night sky. It occurred to me that it was the last heavenly vision which Valerie had seen before she was murdered. I really knew nothing concrete about Valerie Spender. She was a young woman who had entered my life, but had no substance in it. I had been mentioned in her journal. She had known of me. How? My life hadn't crossed over into her life.

I extended my arm toward the heavens, but could grasp nothing except the cold air. I had come alive less than a month ago on a slab of ice and was now taken to the desert to die?

I pounded my fists on the balcony's stone balustrade.

-Stop! Don't harm yourself.

I stopped my useless pounding and leaned against the cold stone. Sweat poured down my neck.

-They did well to choose you.

I turned to look into my hotel room and saw a man's bare legs on my bed. I took a step toward him. He got up with the agility of an athlete. His naked body was etched by shadows and light. He held his hand out toward me.

-Stop. You cannot see my face, Edward Mendez. Do not attempt it, for it is a god whom you see before you. It is a god who speaks to you.

-What is this god's name? Tell me that much, because right now, we're just two naked men on equal terms.

-Not equal. You are my inferior.

-What's your name, pal?

-The deceiver. The warrior whose battles are endless. Look to the tarot card which you stole from Marlena's parlor. You still have an erection. Do I excite you? I can satisfy you.

-You do excite me, but it's not you-

-My strength and my powers of annihilation? Yes. I will satisfy you through annihilation. Come to me!

-No.

-Yes! First your soul...think of it as a shared immortality with me.

-Immortality?

-As your only means of escape from the dread.

-What dread?

-From Marlena's own fears, and from that rather foolish Mass that she will be attempting tomorrow evening.

-Tell me what will happen.

This god moved a step forward and the etched shadows on his body danced.

-The dread? It is nothing but an instant of reckoning when every man, woman, and child will be consumed by the locusts. A few may escape the carnage, but not many. And, they will be dealt with later. But, as I was saying: their hearts will be ripped from their bodies and brought to me so that I may feast upon them. Their remains will be devoured until nothing remains and, then, for a moment, time will have ceased to exist.

This planet will no longer have the binding force of consciousness A new consciousness will be born of my making. Edward Mendez, you excite me.

-Not interested.

-For a moment, if one may use such a term, this world will be devoid of all that lives. Its cities will be empty and there will be a stillness upon this planet that has not been heard before. The dream will come to an end and another dream will begin. The world will be peopled by a new race.

-From where?

-Excellent question! From the very locusts that devour...fresh from the kill!

I lost my erection.

-Yes. It is hideous.

He took another step toward me.

-Don't fear. The sacrifice must be willing.

-But, I come from-

-From where? Beginning to remember, or more accurately put: beginning to prophesy about Howard and Melody and Sean?

He held his arms out to me: muscular and sinewy and beaded with sweat.

-Remembering what you will be? It won't help you. You'll remain here in the unlikely event that I am defeated. And, I will not be defeated by that tenacious woman. I'll help your memory. Time is not of a linear progression which is how you manage to be here in the year 1947. It is how you were slipped through, so to speak, with Yolanda's help. I'll have to kill her for that.

I see you as framed by the beautiful desert night with Diana's bow hovering just above you. You are like a portrait in a gallery that moves when the eye stares at it for too long. Come to me!

-You don't listen too good. No.

-The portrait speaks! Allow me to touch you...to touch the sculpted work which lies within the canvas.

-A new race will be born?

-Yes!

-With souls?

-Of course! However, some with more consciousness than others, but all will be hard and ruthless.

-And, the old souls? the ones that you will have murdered? What happens to them?

-Who cares? Look over your shoulder; but, do not move. Do not disturb the portrait!

All I saw were stars.

-Stars, Edward Mendez...many souls will migrate, but some will choose to stay and brave the ordeal of re-incarnation. Yours will be one of them; but, you may change that.

-I understand now.

-Tell me what you understand.

-Tell me more about yourself.

-I am an ancient...a god to your kind.

-And, to your kind?

-An immortal who was left behind. A cohort of the wandering Jew, for a time. We went our separate ways. He didn't appreciate me.

-Why did you murder Valerie Spender?

-She was a threat to my plans. She understood too much. And, besides, my henchmen did the dirty work: called up from their black hole. I did not soil my own hands. Let me press them upon your warm body.

-Fucking coward! No. Were you Marlena's lover?

-Come to me, and I may answer that.

-No. I'm getting tired of saying that, pal.

I realized then that my vision from before had not been a vision, but a reality. The priestess had been real enough. She had satisfied me so that I would need no further satisfaction no matter what the temptation.

-Who the hell are you?

-A god of an ancient race long gone from this world.

This so-called god held his manhood. His stomach muscles heaved as he let out a scream which pushed me back by a few feet. My bare rump hit the top of the stone railing.

-That was rather nice. Sorry to have made a mess of your floor. I will go now.

-Wait. If I put a bullet through you, pal, would that stop you? It's a simple question, so try answering it.

-No.

-Let me give it a try.

I raced to the bed, but he was too quick for me. He turned around and walked toward and, then, through the damn door.

-Good riddance, you bastard.

CHAPTER FOURTEEN
LOVERS AND ENEMIES

I GOT dressed in a hurry. The sun was on the point of rising and I wanted to speak with Yolanda. I now fancied that I was able to take some educated guesses at a few things. I crossed the hall and knocked on her door. By reflex, I tucked in my black T-shirt and put my sunglasses in my pants pocket.

-Edward! I'm so glad you came. Good. You're wearing your regular street clothes. I didn't like that kaftan. I ordered breakfast for us. It will be here soon. Marlena has tried to keep us apart. I hate her for that. Bitch!

Yolanda's room was almost an exact duplicate of mine. A carpeted hallway led directly into the bedroom. I took a quick look around to make sure that we were alone.

-I'm hungry. But Yolanda, we've got to talk and there's not much time. Susan will come calling for me at any moment and I don't want to arouse her suspicions. I'm surprised she hasn't arrived yet. It's not like her to be late. You can set your watch by her.

-She's nice, but can we trust her? She's Marlena's daughter, you know.

-Agreed. She keeps her mother well informed. Let's sit down.

-Are you in love with Susan?

-No. When I first met her, I thought that I might be.

-Oh? Changed your mind?

-It was more of a paternal feeling. She has no father and her mother…well, you get my drift.

-I understand. What about Gabriel?

-I can't make him out. I've never heard the guy speak. Have you?

-No. Dolores told me once that he only speaks during the Mass. He's strange.

-Agreed. And, have you noticed how Marlena treats him?

-Yes. Like a possessive mother.

-Yes. But only when she's actually speaking to him and giving him orders. She's very loving…almost too loving, if you can guess what I'm hinting at.

-I understand.

-But, whenever we're in any kind of social setting, she ignores Gabriel. It's as if he didn't exist. She doesn't even acknowledge his presence.

-What are you getting at, Edward?

-I'm not so sure, baby. Who is the elder: Susan or Gabriel? Do you know?

-I don't. I think it must be Gabriel. Why?

-They don't look like brother and sister. Susan is kind of plain and looks just a bit like her mother; but Gabriel is handsome and almost-

-Almost what?

-I can't put my finger on it.

-Maybe, he takes after his father.

-I wonder. Just maybe, Susan and Gabriel have different fathers.

-You told me Marlena had a lover. Could he be Gabriel's father?

-With Marlena, anything's possible.

-But, I don't want to talk any more about them. Edward, will we be successful tonight? Do we have a chance?

-Marlena seems to think so.

-But, do you?

-It depends on the moment. If I were a gambling man, I'd be hard pressed on our odds.

-I understand. So what do you want to discuss?

-Your benefactor. Who is he? What's his name, and what does he look like?

-I don't know who he is, not really. He must be wealthy and-

-His name, Yolanda? Don't tell me you don't know it?

-My God, Edward, I don't!

-I believe you. Marlena had a nameless lover, too. What does your benefactor look like?

-What does he look like? Tall and athletic, but…

-Yes?

-But, he shouldn't be, if that makes any sense. He's strong, but always in shadows or standing behind me or talking on the telephone.

-Marlena's nameless lover, your nameless benefactor, and my visitor with no name.

-So, what does it mean? What visitor are you talking about?

-He's one and the same person and another person, as well, if that makes any damned sense. But, the name…he actually mentioned it.

-What name? What man? I'm not understanding this.

-It won't come. It's like having no memory of a future event. It hasn't occurred, yet, so how the hell could you recall something that hasn't even happened yet? Christ!

-Who is this man, Edward, the one who came to you?

-An alien from another world whose race came to the earth millennia ago? An ancient who doesn't have enough sense to die and call it quits? He's manipulating us all, Yolanda: first Marlena, taunting her and, then, using you.

-Why me? And, why Marlena? Why would he tell her anything? Why hasn't he just killed her? I would have.

I laughed out loud at that one.

-Maybe, he can't. Valerie would have been easy pickings for him, but he summoned a bunch of goons to do the job. Why? Why go through all that bother?

-I'll bet he's forbidden to. He's not allowed to do the killing himself.

-That makes sense. It could be some sort of code that he and his kind are bound to. The killing has to be done by indirect means. They can't do the actual killing. Yes! That's what he said: he didn't soil his own hands. But, it doesn't make him any less dangerous, not by a long shot.

-Edward, I've been thinking about this Mass of Marlena's. I think she might have some sort of sacrifice in mind.

-What do you mean?

-Human sacrifice: it's often used in ritual masses.

-I won't let that happen. I won't be a party to murder.

-I'm sure that Marlena doesn't consider it that.

-I do.

-I know that you do; and that's why I love you so. You're a decent man.

-Thanks, baby.

-If the Mass is successful, then what? What about us?

-I'm not rich.

-You could be rich.

-I might be. Still thinking of your skating?

-Yes. I know. I'm pretty selfish. I can't help it.

-Good for you. I'll try to be rich and finance your dream. If it's your dream, then it's mine, too.

-I was hoping that you'd say that.

-Did you have to ask?

-A woman likes to hear these things, Edward. And...

-What is it? Don't hold back, baby; we don't have the time.

-Who was this girl; this Valerie Spender?

-I think she was a clairvoyant of some sort; someone with second sight or a strong gift for prophecy. Maybe, she was having dreams of a future life. You were mentioned in her journal, you know. So was I.

-Me? How? She didn't know me. We never met.

-You told her about my coming to you.

-How could she know that? I didn't even know it.

-Valerie spoke about people in a strange house. These people sounded familiar to me. It's as if I should have *known* these people. It's like awakening from a vivid dream and not remembering anything of it. Damn it!

A knock on the door.

-It's room service, Edward. I'll get it.

-No. I will. Can't be too careful at this point. We've got to stay alive.

Marlena prepared for the Mass. She still hadn't dressed, but there was time enough for that final and crowning touch for a priestess. She had managed to keep the entire landscape empty of people; no one was within human sight but her. The dirt floor of the desert was the temple floor and the coming night was the temple's ceiling of light and darkness. The walls of the temple were the pyramids with the Sphinx as the black guardian of death to all trespassers. It was genius.

Marlena had a visitor.

-Marlena?

-I know you're there. I've been waiting for you. I've been waiting a long time for this.

-Good. You do me quite proud.

-Indeed.

-Are you prepared? Soon all your comrades will be with you. They are coming to you at this moment. You've prepared a magnificent temple, priestess! I congratulate you.

-The ancients were wrong. Armageddon will come early, won't it? Thanks to you.

-My plans had to be pushed up by a few years.

-Why? Are you so anxious to kill us all?

-The answer should be obvious: I don't play fair.

-Neither do I, you bastard. You taught me well. Now, tell me your name so I can spit in your face.

-I have a soft spot for you. Always have.

-Who are you, really? Why are you here? To torment me or to avoid my questions?

-No reason. But, perhaps, I need to tell you something?

-Tell me and get out. I still have to get dressed. One must be prepared for any eventuality. You taught me that much.

-A good magician always is.

-You're beginning to bore me. Say what you have to say and leave.

-Marlena, you are doomed to failure.

-What of it?

-I want you to stop.

-Are you insane? You must be.

-I will have your daughter murdered.

-Kill the bitch. See if I care.

-I will have your beloved Gabriel tortured and slaughtered like a pig.

-One more reason to live and get *you!* And, don't think I won't.

-Stay where you are. I don't want you getting too close…keep me unholy.

-Get out! Leave me like you did years ago. Get out!

-You're sounding so shrill! Why? You will summon me later on because you must. You've no choice. We must meet on the battlefield.

-Don't tempt me because it won't work. I've lived for this moment! It was foretold by the ancients and I intend to fulfill that prophecy.

-It was I who foretold it.

-The outcast Semite. Get out! Liar! Deceiver! If I had my gun on me, I'd kill you here and now.

-I will go.

-And, go straight to *hell!*

CHAPTER FIFTEEN
ARMAGEDDON

THE SUN hovered just to the left of the great pyramid, ripples of orange light were above and below the sacred disc: ripples of inflamed light that formed two opposing triangles in the sky.

-Good evening, Edward. Yolanda? Will you excuse me while I change? Gabriel should be here shortly. Familiarize yourselves with the temple. Edward, I've laid out your garments on the altar; change and try to meditate, if you can.

-No garments for me, Marlena?

-Your street clothes will suffice, my dear. You are the witness to events.

Marlena entered the tent as I looked at the sacred altar. I heard the wind, but couldn't feel it. I looked at my surroundings and saw an ancient temple. The sacred altar faced the east and the stone sarcophagus was opposite in the western quadrant, sixty feet away. To my left were a few silk cushions placed to form a triangle. To my right was another pyramid that reached toward the heavens.

I walked over to the altar and disrobed. In the distance, I saw Gabriel. I took off the rest of my clothes and got into the white kaftan. Yolanda watched me the entire time. Gabriel made slow progress which was just fine by me. I needed the time to collect myself and walk about the temple. As the priest, I must know the ground on which I walk and draw energy from it.

I looked at the sun that would soon descend behind the Great Pyramid, but before that, Diana's bow would rise to meet it. I stopped dead in the center of the temple and knew: was the implication that of magic or reality? Diana's arrow would pierce the sun and herald the destruction.

-Edward, are you all right? Please say that you're not afraid.

-Yolanda, I don't know. What the hell do I know?

I turned and beheld my priestess: Marlena. A complete transformation had been wrought in the space of a few minutes. She looked beautiful, but more than that word could offer. She wore a white robe and sandals. Around her neck, dangling from a gold chain, was a red ruby. She was made-up in the most becoming of ways. In her right hand was the dagger which she gave to me.

-Edward, place this on the altar before the cup and next to the holy book. You are a handsome priest. I knew that you would be.

-Marlena, you look glorious! I almost didn't recognize you.

-Thank you. We must begin immediately- look! Already, the sun and the bow are nearly aligned. Hurry! Place the dagger on the altar and, then, enter the sarcophagus.

Gabriel walked up to us.

-Gabriel, put on your deacon's robe and be quick! Yolanda, sit on the apex of the triangle and do not move from there. Whatever happens outside the magic circle, ignore.

-I understand. I know what to do.

We obeyed our priestess. I placed the dagger before the cup and hurried back to the sarcophagus, patting my gun for reassurance. I entered and closed the lid behind me. I could still sense and hear what was going on outside, though.

Marlena and Gabriel were getting ready to begin. It would be the first time that I'd hear Gabriel speak. Marlena would have to leave the perimeter of the temple and wait just outside of the holy border...dangerous. Yolanda would have to remain quiet and attentive to every word and nuance for she was the witness. Gabriel would be the light-bearer and begin the Mass.

I had a vision: I saw Susan standing in Battery Park in New York City. She was leaning against a rail which separated her from the water's edge. A man approached her. Susan had expected him to come and was ready for him.

-Your mother has given me leave to kill you, Susan.

She stared at this apparition, not quite unbelieving, for she knew her mother only too well. In a challenging voice, she responded.

-When were you given this so-called permission?

-I am being given it now, as we speak. I will explain. I am occupying two places at the same time: a simultaneous appearance, if you will.

-Then, you can tell my darling mother to go to bloody hell and find herself another sacrifice. I'm not willing. I'm an individual and not her slave.

-So many refusals today! Pity! What are you doing here? Why aren't you with your mother at the Mass?

-I really don't know why my mother does anything. I'm sure you know her infinitely better than I do. And, besides, why should I tell you anything?

-Try to make an intelligent guess as to why you are here in New York City.

-I told you.

-Yes? Continue.

-I won't tell you.

-I will kill you.

-Do. I'm not afraid of you or of dying. Why should I be afraid of non-existence?

-You're not afraid to die? I have a great deal of respect for that. Fear doesn't rule your reason. Your emotions are focused and clear. You are not your mother's daughter, for your mother is given to passion and rage. She obsesses.

-Do you have anything else to say except for the obvious?

The vision in New York City left me. I knew why Susan had been sent away. Marlena's enemy and the enemy of mankind was at this moment unfocused and caught off guard. Marlena was playing her cards cleverly. Still, I couldn't rid myself of the feeling that we were doomed to failure. We needed help: an outside force that no one had foreseen must come to our aid now.

At last, Gabriel spoke: it was a soft but strong voice. It was a voice similar to someone else's voice. With a start, I realized something else about him. I didn't really know what the hell he looked like. How was that possible? I'd seen him often enough. I couldn't think about that now. I listened.

-My voice fills the temple of destruction and life. I pray that all may be protected under the golden aegis of Osiris. Osiris! the beautiful god of the temple, hear your son as he speaks your name. Guide your son's movements, focus my thoughts and give unto me my forgotten memory of things toward the infinite. Allow me to serve you so that thine own father's light may not fade from this world of beauty...this world that you have always favored above all your other realms. Ra's chariot now sets in the sky. Allow it to rise on its endless journey still again so that the arc of light may never diminish. Father! make your presence known. Come unto your devoted son!

Again, my vision shifted to New York City and Susan.

-Speak to me, Susan.

-Who are you and where do you come from?

-Again, that question! You know me. We've met before. I was left here by an ancient race whose remnants are now scattered dust in the air that you breathe. I come every six thousand years to wreak havoc or far worse. Although, in truth, I never leave.

-Toward what end? What's the point of it all?

-The awakening of new souls from the heavens and, therefore, the old souls, such as yours, my dear, must journey beyond this pinpoint of light. The giving up of the ghost is not easy.

-So, you rip it from the body, is that it? That must be real easy and delightful work for you and your kind: so easy to murder once you've done it so many times.

-Yes. I knew that you would understand.

-Have others in times past tried to stop you? They must have. They should have!

-I have propositioned them to do so.

-Why did they fail? Or did they even take the bait?

-Emotion got in their way. Their focus became blurred and their intent wavered.

Susan looked about her and knew that there was no earthly way of contacting her mother.

-That's an evasive answer. Can't you do better than that?

-Ah, Susan, notice how still and hot it is even though it is late morning. In a few moments, the cataclysm will begin and no one will be spared.

-And, afterwards? Will there be an afterwards?

-A silence…an oppressive vibration and, then, the metamorphosis from locust to heartless human.

-And, history? How will that be altered?

-An almost unidentifiable ripple in the historic current. The faces will be the same, but the intentions will have changed.

-What kind of a change?

My vision shifted to Gabriel, who was chanting his prayer.

-Oh, beautiful Father send forth your hand-maiden, purify her heart and soul so that none may interfere. Lift the veil which protects this magical circle that we call a temple and allow, for a moment, the veil to part so that your hand-maiden may enter.

I heard footsteps outside my sarcophagus. Marlena had entered the temple. I heard the veil close behind her; but, would it offer us protection?

Something must have heard my unspoken question. At that moment, I heard the beginning of the end. A vibratory and deafening noise infested the air. The droning of wings and the call of the merciless jaws of the locusts. As yet, nothing could be seen in the sky.

The high priestess spoke.

-Oh, ancient father of us all, hear my prayer and answer it. Ancient and most powerful of all gods: the father of Osiris who gave your son the keys to our civilization so that we may endure in consciousness and solemn recognition of you. Save us! Stay the bow of the goddess of the crescent moon! Her arrow of poison and deceit and hallucination is aimed at your very heart.

She is blocking your holy orbit! Annihilate her for this transgression!

But, which god was the evil god? Hadn't Valerie cried out to the same goddess for help? Or, perhaps, an evil hand was guiding that goddess' arrow now? What force could manipulate a god? Was that force with Susan now?

The high priestess turned from the altar and walked toward me. Gabriel followed her as Yolanda looked on. Marlena opened the lid to the stone sarcophagus and signaled Gabriel to remove it to the sand at our feet.

I released myself from the confines of my imprisonment. I walked toward the altar with Marlena behind me followed by Gabriel. Yolanda sat nearby and watched. The sand beneath my bare feet felt hot, but not from the heat of the desert, it was from the energy of this holy place. The pyramids that surrounded us changed in appearance. Their surfaces became smooth and polished and there was a strange written language sculpted on them. The sphinx now had the head of a cat and not that of a man.

The four of us looked up at the sky. The crescent moon and the sun hovered in the sky facing each other. They no longer moved, but were suspended in their orbits.

And, then, we saw it. The dark cloud made its way across the sky, avoiding contact with the warring gods, for neither the sun nor the moon were touched by this unholy plague. The sky grew black and the humming noise was deafening. The plague was coming down upon us. We would be the first to die.

My vision shifted to New York City.

-I must leave you now, Susan, to breathe in the still and warm morning of this pleasant spring day. I need to focus my attention on another matter. I do have my priorities. You will excuse me, of course?

-No. Stay. I have a few more question to ask you. If I'm about to die, you could at least satisfy my intellectual curiosity. There is no God or gods. We attempt to control forces through our mind. It will be explained one day by men of science. Your alleged magic is a more advanced form of technology that we once possessed and will possess, again, one day.

-Look. All of them are leaving their buildings because the silence before the cataclysm is upon them. The most dreaded moment in all of time.

-Talk to me, scientist. You're no god. What utter rubbish!

-What do you mean, Susan? You have my attention.

-This whole ghastly affair is just a beastly joke. And, the biggest joke of all is my mother being at the center of it.

-Why do you say that?

-Don't you question my mother's motives? I do. I always do. She is the most greedy and conniving woman on this planet. And, you believe her purpose is to save humanity? Then, you *are* the fool. I do believe that I hate you for being taken in by her. Fool.

Again, I stood atop the altar and faced Marlena and Gabriel. The wind kicked up into a desert storm. The cloud descended toward us. Yolanda gazed up at the sky, but there was no sky left to see. The hordes were upon us. We were encased in a sarcophagus of hell.

Marlena began her prayer.

-Great Ra, hear my pray...no...my demand! Annihilate your enemy and bring to focus your eternal sun upon this planet. Warm us forever with your radiant light. Look! An inferior points her arrow of poison at you now. Her arrow is possessed by the deceiver. Cast it from the sky!

Marlena and Gabriel stayed in their places with a courage that one doesn't see often in a lifetime.

The hordes of giant locusts pressed in on the magical barrier. Blackness entombed us; but the sun and the moon could still be seen as the locusts darted around these two orbs. The magical circle was caving in as the weight of the plague reached for us. The locusts were hungry.

Yolanda sobbed, but continued her vigil as the witness.

At that moment, a celestial phenomenon occurred: the sun and the moon drew nearer to each other, not as the rational mind of man has studied them, but as two points of energy worshiped by the ancients. The giant locusts moved in fear of them, not daring to be upon the same path of the two gods. The sun and moon would meet and converge and, then, the world cataclysm would begin. Marlena had to stop this by her appeals to the gods. But, how?

The sheer weight of the locusts crushed in on us making breathing more difficult. Our sacred ground was shrinking at a frightening pace. Through the darkness, I saw Marlena take Gabriel's hand and lead him to the altar. He sat upon the summit and his mother commanded him to lie down. She looked up at me and issued the order.

-Edward, send Gabriel on his journey to Osiris.

The sun and crescent moon were almost touching. I could feel the wings of the locusts as they moved closer. I knelt down next to Gabriel and stripped him of his robe. Naked, he lay upon the altar. Marlena handed me the blade.

Yolanda screamed, but remained where she was.

I knelt down beside Gabriel as the altar trembled. And, then, another figure knelt down before me. It was an etheric figure who traversed through the hordes of locusts to place a gold medallion upon Gabriel's chest: a medallion with a golden arrow emblazoned on it. The ghost of Valerie knelt before me as I raised the blade and struck the death blow. She guided my hand. I didn't want to do this. The boy didn't cry out, but the golden arrow became blinding to look at as Gabriel's blood touched it. Marlena, Yolanda, and I turned away from its brilliance. It was this brilliance which radiated out to the hordes of locusts…killing them…each one bursting into flames and falling to the earth. Their death cries were a horror. The radiant light of Ra had defeated mankind's enemy.

Valerie's astral body passed through my body and Marlena's. Gabriel would be safe with her. Valerie's courage and Gabriel's heroism: simple virtues to help destroy the insidious vice of an evil.

The wind stopped as the hordes dropped dead on the desert floor leaving us in a clearing surrounded by the smell of decay. The silence which followed was an almost intoxicating relief.

Marlena and I looked skyward. Yolanda went to the body of Gabriel. The sun and the moon were where they had been: the celestial fire setting into the horizon and the lunar crescent rising skyward toward its zenith.

I jumped down from the altar.

-Good job, Edward. Gabriel was my beloved son, but one must make the most dire of sacrifices and- oh!

Marlena and I turned around and stared at an approaching figure. It looked like a man, but it could not be a man. The specter raised its arms. It approached us too quickly.

Yolanda looked up and screamed.

-Edward! He's the one!

We backed away. Marlena and Yolanda were behind me, not daring to take their eyes off the specter who was almost upon us.

-Edward, we mustn't leave the perimeter of the temple or we're all doomed. We have to face this and destroy it. My enemy doesn't know when to give up.

Yolanda made to run.

-Edward, stop her! We need her energy and three must form the triangle.

I grabbed my girlfriend around the waist and this calmed her down. She stayed where I placed her. I turned to Marlena in anger and frustration.

-I thought we'd won. Did we kill your son for nothing?

-We did win. But, my enemy won't accept defeat. He's cheating.

-Now, what?

-The blade? You still have the blade, don't you?

Yolanda answered her.

-Edward, it's in the pocket of your kaftan. I saw you put it there. Take it out!

Marlena smiled with satisfaction.

-Good. Then, use it. Kill the bastard!

The specter was upon us. He raised his arms and motioned for Marlena to come to him.

-You've won, murderous bitch. But, now a lover's trophy for me: your miserable body atop the pyramid. My minions will place you on the pinnacle of that ancient structure.

-Where's my daughter, Susan?

-A clever ploy, Madame, that: a divergence of my attention, diverting the focus of my intent. You played your cards well. The disease has been prevented, but its source, you failed to cut down.

Marlena, Yolanda, and I raced along the perimeter of the temple. We couldn't stop because it didn't stop. But, just maybe, a bullet would stop it. I took my pistol out and fired at it. To my surprise, it staggered back a few feet. It looked up at me.

-A primitive weapon, Edward Mendez. I expected better from you.

-How about another primitive bullet?

I fired at point blank range, but this time my bullet had only a negligible effect. It'd been ready for it.

-You've lost the element of surprise. Now, throw away your weapon like a good boy.

I fired the last three bullets and these had no effect at all. Yolanda got my attention.

-Edward, it has to be the dagger. There's no other way.

It was closing in on us. It spoke to Marlena.

-Marlena, you won't die too quickly. You will feed the carrion until every piece of flesh is stripped away from your rotten body. A small consolation, but an enjoyable one. It will be a diverting entertainment to soothe me. I'll let the vultures do the actual killing while I remain a mere spectator.

It lunged for Marlena, but she was too quick for it. She dodged the blow and ran back toward the altar. It ran after her and I ran after it; but, it turned around and hit me on the right side of my head. I went down in agony on to my knees. Yolanda embraced me.

Marlena reached the altar. I tried to get to my feet. Yolanda tried to help me up. We both staggered. I could feel blood streaming from my right eye. Everything took on a red haze, but the blood actually enhanced my vision.

The specter grabbed Marlena; but, she was strong and the two of them went down to the ground wrestling. Slowly, though, it was wearing her down.

I got to my feet with Yolanda's help and took the blade from my sleeve. I ran across the sands toward the two combatants. I was almost there when the specter raised Marlena against the altar. I plunged the dagger into its neck, separating the spinal cord at the base of the skull. The cut was clean and quick. It let go of Marlena. She dropped to the ground. In its death throes, it turned to look at me. I recognized it as the god-like figure that had appeared in my hotel room.

-I know you, Edward Mendez. Perhaps, I was not the enemy you thought.

-No? Then, who the hell are you, pal?

-How could I expect you to recognize me? No matter. The life force is leaving me.

It crumpled to the ground and deteriorated into dust. The three of us stared at the heap of dust that the wind was now blowing away. I turned to face my priestess.

-What did he mean by that, Marlena? Why would I recognize him?

-I've an idea, but we've no time to discuss it now. He's a liar, anyway. And, does it matter? I've won. And, for the first time in over twenty five years, I can breathe with ease without looking over my shoulder. My vigilance is over, for now.

-Oh? And, now what?

-An excellent question, Yolanda. First, we must clear things up here. The police may come by and ask some awkward questions. We must have our answers prepared. We'll bury my son at the base of the pyramid. You and Edward may do that, but be quick. I'll gather up the altar things and join you as soon as I can. When things settle down, we'll head back to New York and join Susan.

Yolanda and I carried Gabriel's body toward the base of the great pyramid. The boy felt light as I carried him with care.

-Yolanda?

-What is it? Is Gabriel too heavy for you?

-No. He's light as the proverbial feather. It's just…that pressure on my finger is gone. I don't feel it anymore.

-What pressure?

-I can't explain it. It's just gone. And, that subtle fragrance? That's gone, too. It's a relief. I feel whole, again. It's as if I'm completely my own man now.

-I thought you always were.

-And, my past, Yolanda, it's starting to come back. Christ! I feel like a man with a past and a future to look forward to. What's the matter, baby? Am I coming on too strong?

-No. It's not that. It's just- Edward, I'm still afraid.

-Afraid of what? It's over.

-Is it? I'm not so sure about that. Something doesn't feel right. Marlena doesn't look too upset about her precious son being killed.

-I noticed that, too. That is kind of strange, now that you mention it. I expected a little more emotion from her.

-Edward, you were hinting that Gabriel's father might have been that thing you just killed?

-Yes. You don't think so?

-I think you're right; and when his blood was spilled, it wasn't ordinary blood.

-And, that's what triggered the medallion?

-That must be it. Maybe, Marlena loved and hated Gabriel. She loved him because he *was* her son and hated him because that alien was his actual father.

-We'll have to talk about this later at the hotel, baby. I think you're right on the money, though. But, right now, let's get this burial over with. God only knows how many Egyptian laws we're breaking.

My vision shifted to New York City and Susan.

-I have just been killed.

-I beg your pardon?

-I must retreat now and count my losses. I'm not accustomed to doing that.

-What in the world are you talking about? Retreat to where? What's actually happened?

-Your mother, Susan, has won. That hag has had her way and done what no other human being has been able to do on this planet. I have been defeated upon the battlefield. Edward has given up a future incarnation by coming to this time and place and helping Marlena to succeed thanks to that bitch, Yolanda. As for myself, a part of me has been destroyed. I go to the other part of the glyph which is now empty. I'll pour myself one last drink at Howard's bar.

EPILOGUE

-YOU ALL know me. I'm the gatherer of those people to this accursed spot: the point of darkness that was disguised as Howard's bar in the midst of that sprawling metropolis, New York City, which really wasn't anywhere. The whiskey is hard and good and there's plenty of it to keep me company for a good long stretch. I'll need it.

One shot.

Another shot.

One more shot.

Fucking good liquor.

Melted ice going down the throat with the stain of sin on it. Lovely.

-Now what was I saying? Oh yeah. I'm waiting for another chance and another time to set the plague loose upon that world and that time will come. It will come! Edward and Marlena won't be around to stop me. That woman is one cunning bitch. And, Edward's one crack shot. Those bullets hurt. Maybe I'm finally acquiring mortality? Maybe.

He drank straight from the bottle and finished it. And, just for kicks, he flung the empty bottle through the front window. The glass shattered on to the pavement in silence because there was no one in this phantasmic world to hear it.

-And, to think that all of those gifted and interesting and scared shitless people are gone. Pity! You might say that they were never here to begin with, but that isn't quite accurate. Somewhere in the folds of time and space, their brief stay here has been noted. I hope that they liked me. Melody didn't because she knew that I was a liar which is a part of my trade. Did she suspect the truth? I suspect that she did. I know that Howard liked me in his own arrogant and egotistical manner; and, to think that he will never exist. Well, he won't exist as Howard. I must make a toast to him. I'll just open up another bottle of whiskey…this one will do.

-Howard! with love, from your friend, Sean, the Irishman!

The End

COMING SOON:

NIGHT DRIFTER:
An Edward Mendez, P.I. Thriller

BOOK II

THE OUTCASTS

Howard Winter - a young man who likes to drink whiskey and manipulate people. His bar is mankind's last refuge against the Time Deceiver.

Sean - an Irishman who likes tending bar and telling lies and hovering in the background. He also likes to drink, like his best friend, Howard.

Irene MacDonald - a psychic who enjoys being at the center of attention even when she's groping in the dark.

Rose MacDonald - Irene's older sister, who is comical and perceptive. She doesn't trust Howard or his motives.

Max Dexter - a man with a drinking problem who doesn't seem to care that the world may be coming to an end.

Yvonne Duval - an alcoholic who knows something of the unfolding events, but is too frightened to realize their import.

Becky - an "innocent" who's the first victim of the evil surrounding Howard's bar.

Michael - a teenager caught up in events who thinks that Howard is nothing but a trouble-maker.

Abraham - a quiet but arrogant man who won't share his knowledge with anyone.

Oshido Tsu - a man of wisdom who knows how to ask the right questions. He suspects the true motive behind Becky's murder.

Melody - a "sensitive" to the occult world who feels drawn to Howard. She also fears for him and his safe return to the present.

THE GAME PLAYERS: 1947

Edward Mendez - a man with a forgotten past and a future which may not last beyond the next few days. He is mankind's last hope for survival; but can he trust the one person who can help him?

Yolanda Estravades - a beautiful figure skater who's in love with Edward. She knows dangerous people…and a few of them want to kill her.

Marlena Lake - a complex woman of knowledge, resourcefulness, and cunning. She "enlists" Edward's help in fighting an old enemy.

Dolores Sarney - a friend of Yolanda's and a member of Marlena's group who's the second victim of the Time Deceiver.

Rosamund Spender - a possessive and bitter woman whose sister, Valerie, was just murdered.

Susan Broder - Marlena's intelligent and practical daughter who doesn't believe in the occult world as her mother does.

Erich Manfred - a young Nazi who was unable to save his doomed girlfriend, Valerie.

Gabriel Broder - Marlena's son who is a silent but strong young man of few words.

The Priest - a monster from the depths of hell who seeks redemption through Marlena.

Dan - a man who works in Edward's office building and likes spying on people.

Valerie Spender - a clairvoyant who predicts the coming Armageddon, but is helpless to stop it.

ABOUT THE AUTHOR

Gerard Denza has worked in the Publicity Dept. at Random House and Little, Brown, and Company in New York City. He's worked with such authors as Pete Hamill, Arthur C. Clarke, Willie Morris, Pat Booth, and Kevin and Todd Berger. He's the author and director of six Off Off Broadway plays that include:

ICARUS, MAHLER: THE MAN WHO WAS NEVER BORN, THE DYING GOD: A VAMPIRE'S TALE, SHADOWS BEHIND THE FOOTLIGHTS, and THE HOUSEDRESS.

His noir play, EDMUND: THE LIKELY, has been recorded for radio broadcast Mr. Denza is a graduate of Fordham University at Lincoln Center where he majored in psychology.

He lives in New York City and is hard at work on his next novel: NIGHT DRIFTER: AN EDWARD MENDEZ, P. I. THRILLER.